CHARMED TO DEATH

MAGIC HAPPENS
BOOK 2

YASMINE GALENORN

A Nightqueen Enterprises LLC Publication

Published by Yasmine Galenorn

PO Box 2037, Kirkland WA 98083-2037

CHARMED TO DEATH

A Magic Happens Novel

Copyright © 2023 by Yasmine Galenorn

First Electronic Printing: 2023 Nightqueen Enterprises LLC

First Print Edition: 2023 Nightqueen Enterprises

Cover Art & Design: Ravven

Art Copyright: Yasmine Galenorn

Editor: Elizabeth Flynn

A Nightqueen Enterprises LLC Publication

Published in the United States of America

ACKNOWLEDGMENTS

Welcome to the Magic Happens world—the world of Marquette Sanders.

Thanks to my usual crew: Samwise, my husband, Andria and Jennifer—without their help, I'd be swamped. To the women who have helped me find my way in indie, you're all great, and thank you to everyone. To my wonderful cover artist, Ravven, for the beautiful work she's done and my editor, Elizabeth Flynn, who's always ready to jump in and curb my love of ellipses, and Jade, who has an eagle eye.

Also, my love to my furbles, who keep me happy. My heart is over the rainbow with my Rainbow Girls, and here in the present with our current babies. My most reverent devotion to Mielikki, Tapio, Ukko, Rauni, and Brighid, my spiritual guardians and guides. My love and reverence to Herne, and Cernunnos, and to the Fae, who still rule the wild places of this world. And a nod to the Wild Hunt, which runs deep in my magick, as well as in my fiction.

You can find me through my website at **Galenorn.com** and be sure to sign up for my **newsletter** to keep updated on all my latest releases and to access the VIP section of my website, which has all sorts of perks on it! You can find my advice on writing, discussions about the books, and general ramblings on my **YouTube Channel** and my **blog**. If you liked this book, I'd be grateful if you'd leave a review—it helps more than you can think.

Brightest Blessings,

-The Painted Panther-
-Yasmine Galenorn-

WELCOME TO CHARMED TO DEATH

November brings with it the annual windstorms, but another kind of storm is brewing. All over town, people are becoming unhappy with their partners. At Shadow Magic, we're getting more requests than we can handle for love potions, Be-True charms, Reveal-Cheater spells, and anything you can think of to do with romance and its vagaries.

Granny and I know that something sinister is afoot, but we aren't sure what. Until Dagda Bruin—the chief of police—asks us for help.

We discover a full-scale magical virus going on that's causing broken hearts, fights between jilted lovers, and scandalous affairs everywhere. As we try to figure out what's going on, one fight leads to murder, and the race is on to discover not only the source of this mayhem, but a cure for what's ailing the lovelorn of Terameth Lake. And if we don't move soon, the body count's going to rise as tempers and infidelities escalate.

Reading Order for the Magic Happens Series:

CHAPTER ONE

I woke up to find Midnight staring down at my face. She had planted herself on my chest, and was now nose to nose with me, her whiskers tickling my cheeks. I squinted at her, trying to decide whether I had heard the alarm go off. I didn't think so, but Midnight had taken to jumping on my chest as soon as the alarm rang. Sunshine, however, was proving to be a lazy little furball, who would saunter down for breakfast when he was ready.

"Is it morning already?" I yawned, reaching out with my right hand to grab for my phone.

It's close enough, Midnight said. *And I'm hungry, so get up and feed us!*

Spoken like a real cat.

"Remember what I told you? Unless it's an emergency, you don't get to wake me up in the middle of the night just to feed or pet you. Not unless you're feeling really upset." I knew better than to truly expect them to respect my wishes. Midnight and Sunshine were cats, after all, even if they were familiars. And they epitomized the nature of "cat" perfectly.

1

It is *an emergency. The food dish is empty. And I think Granny is outside.*

I snorted, glancing at my phone. It was seven forty-five, and my alarm wasn't set to go off until eight-fifteen. But I knew my chances of getting any more sleep were null and void. I turned off my alarm, set the phone back on the night-stand, and—holding Midnight around the tummy—I slowly scooted my way up to lean back against the headboard.

"All right, you win." I knew how dangerous those two words were when spoken to a cat, but I didn't have the heart to tell her no. "Okay, I'm getting up. You go wake up your brother and go wait by the food bowl. I'll be down as soon as I've showered and dressed."

Midnight let out a long-suffering sigh, then turned and jumped off the bed, marching toward the door. If she had been human, her shoulders would be sinking right now and she would probably give me an injured look. As it was, she reached where she thought she couldn't see me just outside the door, and then I heard her thunder off down the stairs. Oh, the drama of it all!

DOWNSTAIRS, I FOUND COFFEE WAITING FOR ME, ALONG with a couple homemade sausage muffins ready to heat up in the microwave. As I settled down at the table with my breakfast, along with a massive cup of milk-and-sugar infused coffee, I glanced over at the cats. They were scarfing down breakfast so fast that it occurred to me I should put something like a golf ball in their dish to keep them from eating so fast. Both of them were chunking up, and their coats were sleek and beautiful.

Turning back to my phone, I pulled up the news head-lines. Ever since I had left the Crown Magika, I had tried to keep up on the inside events going on there. But I was no longer in the loop and, even if someone there thought to inform me, they'd be breaking the rules. So I flipped over to the Terameth Lake Gazette website and scanned the headlines.

Avis Trenton had been arrested again, this time for public nudity. She had gotten drunk and jumped naked into the town square fountain. I grimaced. Avis was fifty-eight and quickly becoming one of the town drunks. Her antics were famous, but left me feeling sad because Avis had crumbled when her husband ran off with the gardener, taking every cent he could lay his hands on. She was alone, she couldn't afford the mortgage, she had no job other than being a spectacular mother, and now she was left to care for three kids under the age of ten with no help from their father.

In other news, the Jenkinson cows had broken out and there was a massive roadblock on Belfry Drive. The website hadn't been updated in half an hour so there was a good chance it had been cleared by now, but I made a note that when I went down to the shop, I'd avoid that route.

And then another article caught my eye. I scrolled down to it. Sometime during the night, someone—or something—had scratched up Molly Meagher's car. The picture was appalling. Long scrapes dug into the side of the driver's door had left massive scratches in the metal, and they were so big that I knew they hadn't come from any mountain lion or bear that I could think of.

The microwave beeped and I carried my muffins back to the table, where I sat down. As I stuffed one into my mouth, I realized it was too hot and I waved my hand briskly in front of my lips to cool the heat that spread through my tongue and my mouth.

As the heat dissipated, I stared at the picture of Molly's car. What the hell had attacked it? Maybe a saber-toothed tiger was running around the village? Considering the things that came out of Hell's Thicket, I wouldn't be surprised if it was something other than just a pissed-off bear or some teen wearing a Wolverine claw set.

After I finished glancing through the news, I picked up the stack of mail. As I leafed through it, two were easily recognizable as bills. Three pieces were for Granny, and three were for me. Mine were stiff, probably birthday cards. My birthday was Saturday—on the nineteenth. I tucked them into my purse. The ones for Granny, I left by her side of the table.

Yawning, I chugged down the coffee and readied myself to leave for the day. I had promised Granny I would take today at the shop if she would take tomorrow for me. Verity was throwing a party for me on Saturday night, but tomorrow night was the first date I'd agreed to in a couple years, and I wasn't sure exactly how I felt about it.

Tomorrow night, Colton was taking me out to a movie and a late dinner. I had sworn up and down to myself that I wouldn't date again, at least not for a long time. Now here I was, breaking my vow.

But people could change their minds, *right?*

I liked to think I was calm and collected, but beneath the surface, I was nervous. I had *no clue* how to act on a date. I didn't even know *how* to date anymore. I hadn't gone out with anybody in years, and the last time I had, it had been the breakup from hell. She had hurt me so bad that I had sworn off both men and women and focused on my work to the exclusion of anything else. But when Colton had asked me out, he was so calm that it soothed my fears.

Sure, I was fifty-two, almost fifty-three, and I didn't want a steady boyfriend, but the thought of having dinner with a good friend and possibly, maybe, dinner leading to a kiss made me smile.

And Dagda Bruin could go suck lemons.

THE NIGHT BEFORE, WHEN DAGDA FOUND OUT I WAS going to go out with Colton, he had blown up and picked a fight with me. I couldn't figure out why he was being such an ass. Dagda had a girlfriend, and I had no interest in dating him. We butted heads in the worst of ways, and he was acting like an older brother.

I had told him in no uncertain terms that "thank you but I *have* a brother and I wouldn't listen to *him*, so I'm not about to listen to you. Tend to your own garden. I'm perfectly capable of making my own decisions."

He had stormed out, a brooding look on his face.

Granny tried to smooth my ruffled feathers. "The two of you fight worse than anybody I know," she had said. "It reminds me of when you and your brother Billy lived here."

"I don't know *why* Dagda rubs me the wrong way," I said. "I don't dislike him, but I sure like to needle him. He's so quick to blow up."

"I wonder," Granny said. She pulled out her computer and ran some computations, then—sputtering—she leaned back and laughed her head off. "Okay, *that* answers it. No wonder the two of you butt heads. You're a Scorpio with an Aries moon and he's a Virgo with a Capricorn moon. That alone ensures the pair of you will be sparring for the rest of your lives. Just be careful that you don't let it go too far. I can see an argument blowing up big someday to where you might not be able to mend the rift."

Sparring partners or not, I didn't have time to mull over my fractious friendship with Dagda.

"I'm not going to be the one to constantly keep the peace.

I don't think of him as a frenemy, but we're close. Anyway, I don't have the time to worry about it."

I SHOOK AWAY THOUGHTS OF THE ARGUMENT AND stretched. I wanted to get in a workout before hitting the shop, so I said goodbye to the kittens, slung my workout bag over my shoulder, and headed out for the day. Granny was still asleep, and I didn't want to wake her. She had put in a late night helping a friend clear a ghost out of her house and needed her rest.

As I headed to the truck, keys in hand, the skies opened and rain lashed down sideways, soaking me before I could make it to my truck. I slid into the driver's seat and slammed the door, but I was already drenched to the bone. If I'd been in a T-shirt, I could have won a wet T-shirt contest. I wiped the water off my forehead, glancing in the rearview mirror to make certain my eye makeup was still intact. Satisfied, I slid the key into the ignition and eased out of the driveway.

Chaz waved as I entered the gym. The owner was a buff young man who had asked me out about a dozen times. He was too young for me, though, and the last time he had asked, I told him firmly but politely to stop. I liked Chaz. He was fun and he was a good personal trainer, but I lectured him on crossing boundaries. He apologized, and we were good. I chalked his eagerness up to the fact that he was lonely. His ex-girlfriend had left him with an inferiority complex, and he seemed out to prove that he wasn't a loser.

"Hey Marquette," he said. "What are you working on today?"

"Legs. I had a PT appointment. Therapist says I'm focusing on cardio too much, and that I need to build the muscle around my knee again or it could blow out."

"What kind of exercises does your therapist want you to do?" Chaz asked.

"I need to do some knee-friendly weight-bearing exercises. While I change, if you could think up a few for me, that would help." I handed him the piece of paper from my therapist. "Here's a few she recommended. It will give you an idea of what I need."

By the time I had finished donning my workout gear, Chaz had come up with a simple routine for me. Hopefully, it would help. My knee had gone out on me in September and it was still hurting. If I didn't get the muscles strengthened up soon, I'd have more problems than just aching when the rains hit. We put in a grueling forty-five minutes and, after thanking him for his help, I hit the showers, changed, and headed down to the shop.

SO, I'M MARQUETTE SANDERS, AND I WAS ONE OF THE TOP agents for the Crown Magika. But earlier in the year I ended up on the wrong side of the asphalt. I was taking a turn at around a hundred and forty to a hundred and fifty miles per hour, chasing down a rogue vampire, when my motorcycle skidded out from under me, catching my heel and dragging me long enough to shatter the bones in my leg. Given how easily I could have lost my life, I consider myself lucky.

Though I heal quickly, given that I'm witchblood, it was soon apparent I'd never fully be whole again. I lost my job with the Crown Magika. They offered me a desk job, but I couldn't face the transition. I loved my work too much. So I walked away. I sold Duchess—my motorcycle—and resigned myself to a slower life as a civilian.

Now I work with Granny—my goddess-mother—in her magical shop, Shadow Magic. In an unexpected twist, I'm now also working pro bono for the police department, helping out on investigations when they need an extra hand. Dagda Bruin—the chief of police—is so strapped on his budget that he's given me a special investigator's license. No, life isn't turning out the way I wanted it to, but I'm learning to adapt. And I'm finding that happiness is a choice, rather than some elusive prize to be won.

I NO SOONER OPENED THE DOORS WHEN ONE OF OUR regular customers rushed through. Charisma Mathers was twenty-five years old, with a waifish body and boobs that were way too big for her frame. They were about as natural as her hair color. While I still had the same blond hair I'd been born with, her blond hair was definitely from a bottle. There was nothing wrong with that, except it didn't look good on her. She had skin fit for a redhead, or maybe a rich mahogany.

"Hey Charisma, how goes it?" I took my place behind the counter as she dropped her purse on the glass.

"I need your help. I'm frantic!" Her eyes were wide, and by her breathy voice, I could tell she was panicked.

"What's going on?"

As flamboyant as she looked, Charisma wasn't one given over to being a drama queen. In fact, she was one of the smartest women I'd met in Terameth Lake.

"I think Jake's having an affair. I need something to reveal the truth."

"*Jake?*" I stared at her. She was going out with a man who was devoted to her, and I couldn't possibly see him running around on the side. Then again, I didn't have that much experience in the romance department. "Did he tell you that he was?"

She shook her head. "No, he didn't. But I can feel it. I

know he's up to something." She slapped the top of the counter, and I gently grabbed her hand.

"You don't want to do that to a glass display case. While the glass is strong, you don't need to smash your fist through it. Now tell me, why do you think he's sneaking around? What signs have you noticed?"

She heaved out a sigh, tears glistening in the corners of her eyes. "He's been late the last three nights, and he doesn't have any excuse for where he was. He hasn't even said work's being a problem. He just tells me to quit nagging and to give him his space. He's never said anything like that to me before."

That did sound odd. But there could be a lot of reasons behind his behavior.

"Are you sure he's not in any financial trouble, or maybe having problems at work? He could have a lot of stress on his shoulders." Work stress could be a real bear for a lot of people. And finances had broken up more relationships than sex.

Charisma stared down the countertop. She worried her lip. "The truth is, Jake and I've been through the wringer over the past couple years. We've been trying to conceive, and for three years it just wouldn't happen. Then, early this year I got pregnant, only to have a miscarriage. We pulled through, and he was there for me when I needed it. I don't know what I would have done without him. Then his mother died a month after that—in April. I stood by him and did my best to focus on his needs."

"That's a lot for the two of you to handle in such a short time," I said.

"Yes, but by August, we were feeling in a clear headspace again. We've been together ten years, Marquette. I *know* Jake. If he was having trouble on his job, he would tell me. We haven't kept secrets from each other in years. No, this feels different. He's keeping something from me, and I can't help but think it's another woman. I've never been this worried about our relationship."

I thought about it for a moment, then asked, "Would you like a tarot reading? It might be able to sort out some things. Then we can decide what direction you need to move in."

She gave me a little shrug. "I suppose. Do you have any time today?"

"I can see you at four." We scheduled certain times during the day for readings. If other customers came in during that time, there was a sign on the counter along with a bell in case they needed help. But we tried to keep the tarot appointments to the beginning and end of the day, so our customers got used to the flow. When Granny and I were both here, it didn't matter as much. One of us could work the counter while the other gave readings.

"I'll be back then. Thanks, Marquette. I know I'm right, but I suppose I should get some sort of confirmation first, and a reading would be the best way." She left a little calmer than when she had entered the shop, but she still looked dejected.

I penciled her into the schedule, and then looked around. The herbs needed restocking, and I should probably rearrange a couple of the displays so they'd look better. But before I could make it to the stockroom, the door bells jingled again and Jillian stomped in, looking ready to kill.

She ran the cat café next door. I had adopted Midnight and Sunshine from her, and we had become good friends.

"Hey—" I started to say, but then I read her energy and stopped. Something was wrong. She was shooting off enough sparks to start a wildfire. I hurried around the counter. "What's wrong?"

"Henry broke it off with me last night. Well, good for him. He's an asshole and I want to blast him into outer space." Jillian headed over to the table in the corner and sat down. She rested her elbows on the table. "I can't believe I ever thought he was one of the good ones. Crap, how can men turn into jerks so easily? I feel like an idiot, thinking he was worth spending my time on. I should have just followed my gut and focused on the business and my cats." A widow, Jillian had resisted dating for over five years. In October she had met Henry, who seemed pretty nice, and they had been dating for a little over a month.

"Did he give you a reason?" I wondered if Venus was retrograde, or whatever planet it was that ruled over romance and relationships. I wasn't the person to ask about astrology. Granny handled that aspect of the shop's magical services.

"Oh, he told me *why*, all right. He told me I had a *fat ass*, that I should go on a diet because he doesn't like *poking so much padding*. I called him a fuckhead and told him to take his lame-ass shriveled-up old dick and hit the road."

I blinked. Well, *that* was unexpected. I'd pegged Henry for a decent guy and I was usually a good judge of people. But apparently, not in this case. "What did he say?"

"He laughed and said that nobody else would even give me the once-over at my age, and that I should be grateful he showed me any attention at all."

I cringed. That wasn't good. "So, he's still alive?"

Jillian grimaced. "Unfortunately, yes. I slapped him, and then he called me a whale, and then I threw a pie at him and he left." She let out a sigh. "I think I'm more angry at myself for ignoring the signs than at him for what he said. I can't believe he duped me, Marquette! I feel like an idiot—like some angsty teenager crying over a two-timing boyfriend."

My first instinct was to hunt him down and beat him up, but I resisted. Even with the residue from my injuries, I was in far better shape than he was, and I could have clocked him a good one before he knew what was coming. But violence wasn't the answer in this case, and I could help Jillian better by listening than by acting all super-heroine.

"What a fucking jerk. I can't believe he said those things to you. Well, I *can* believe it, I just don't want to. I'm so sorry, but you're better off without him."

"Oh I know, I really do. And I'm doing my best to resist the impulse to ask you for a poppet so I can stick a few pins in it. I would love to deflate his ego, preferably in front of someone important." She looked up, shaking her head. "What's wrong with some of these men? I know women can be horrible too, but it seems like more of my female friends end up with the short end of the stick than the guys they've been with."

"You're preaching to the choir," I said. "That's why I don't do relationships."

"Yeah, but you're going on a date tomorrow night," she said, her scowl lifting a little. "I just hope you have better luck than I did."

"You know that *all* I'm looking for is an enjoyable evening. Colton is very nice, and he's an extremely talented witch, but I don't expect it to go anywhere. We're just going out to get some dinner and watch a movie." It occurred to me that Jillian would make a great girlfriend, but I knew she didn't swing that way and I'd never press in where it was unwelcome.

"I know that's what you say, but is that how you *really* feel?"

I thought about it for a moment, testing my internal bullshit meter. It rang true, for the most part. I did detect a little bit of hope that I hadn't expected, so I said, "Ninety percent true. There's a little part of me that hopes it turns into a second date. I can't truthfully say I'm interested in a relationship, but dating can be fun. I've had my share of partners over the years. Though the last one left me with a bitter taste in my mouth. *So bitter* I've been gun-shy ever since."

"Do you ever think you want to get married?" she asked.

That, I could answer without hesitation. "Nope. Not a chance. I've never aspired to wear a wedding dress, nor to walk down the aisle, be it with a man or a woman. I'm set in my ways. Granny and I get along because we leave each other alone for the most part. We're not trying to change each other, or control each other, and we're not in a relationship. Well, other than she's my goddess-mother and we're friends."

"That makes sense. You've always lived alone, haven't you?" Jillian asked.

I nodded. "All of my adult life, so this roommate business is new. The Crown Magika provided us with apartments. I do want to buy myself a house in the next year or two, but not for a while yet. But when I do, it will be furnished *my* way, painted in the colors *I* choose, and kept in the fashion *I* prefer. I like companionship, but I don't want a partner."

"Are you sure you're not protesting too much?"

I laughed. "No, I've just had to defend my choices over the years, so I get a little pushy about it. If I had a dollar for every person who's told me that I'm going to regret not having children or being married when I'm on my deathbed, I'd be fucking rich." I was about to ask her if she wanted something cold to drink when the door opened and Dagda came in. Before I could say anything, he motioned for me to follow him into the storeroom.

"Come on, I need to talk to you."

"I'll be right back," I told Jillian, narrowing my eyes as I followed Dagda. "Dude, *ask* before you drag me into our private storeroom," I started to say, sitting down at the lunch table. He frowned at me like I was a gnat, and I let out a snort. "Seriously, you need to learn some manners."

"Never mind that. Something weird is going down. I have

no idea what to make of it." The look on his face silenced my irritation.

"What's happened?" I was worried now, and decided to ignore his rudeness.

"All five of our jail cells are full. We've broken up five different fights today, and I'm not talking about scuffles. I'm talking about all-out brawls and fistfights. And it's barely ten-thirty. I've got every car out there trying to keep up with the list of people who are mixing it up. The 911 system has logged more calls this morning than it's had the past month." He sounded both exasperated and confused.

"What the hell?" Whatever it was, it didn't sound normal. "What are people fighting about?"

"That's what gets me. Two fights were over a woman. I also had to break up a domestic violence incident where a wife was beating up her husband. She claims he was cheating on her. The fourth call involved a pervert trying to crawl in a woman's bedroom window. And the last one, well, a couple got into it in Melton's Hardware, where they began to tear up the aisles and throw stuff at each other." He looked positively bewildered.

"Well, that's different." I scratched my ear. Dagda did have a problem.

He gave me a beleaguered look. "Is there a full moon? Is everybody just going stir-crazy because of the rain? The holidays are coming up, maybe that's spurring this on? Whatever the case, I wasn't kidding when I asked about the moon. Do you know if there's any astrological reason behind this? Because for the life of me, we're running out of places to put people."

CHAPTER TWO

I stared at him for a moment, trying to think of a proper response. Sometimes, coincidences were coincidences, and while this sounded fucknut crazy, there *could* be a logical explanation. Just what it might be, I had no idea. But maybe he was right. Maybe something *was* going on with the stars. I wasn't the person who could answer that, though.

"Why don't you give Granny a call? She's the one who understands astrology. Or you can try one of the other astrologers in town. Carolyn White Oak runs an excellent astrology service, from what people have told me."

Dagda stared at me for a moment. "You really can't help me?"

I shook my head. "Really, truly. I can tell you when the moon is full and when it's new, but without looking at an ephemeris, I have no idea what's up. And even if I were to look it up, I wouldn't be able to interpret the information. We cast certain spells based on the phases of the moon, but I'm not conversant with the stars. It's just not my thing."

"I thought all witches knew all about astrology and horoscopes and those sort of things." He was definitely grumpy, all right.

"Just like all bear shifters eat honey and steal picnic baskets, and are patriarchal and pushy?" I paused, rolling my eyes. "Actually, that's not a good example. Most of you *are* patriarchal and pushy. And who doesn't like honey? Or a good picnic basket?"

"You know very well that I respect women—"

"Dagda, I don't doubt it." I cut him off. "But have you learned to cook yet?"

Dagda couldn't boil water. He seemed to feel cooking was beneath him—*women's work*, although he was, like most men, willing to man a grill when asked. Even his girlfriend and mother were browbeating him to at least learn how to make a grilled cheese sandwich and open a can of tomato soup.

"Eh, shuddup."

"You catch more flies with honey than vinegar, dude." I crossed my arms, leaning back in my chair. "I've got to get back out front."

He heaved a long sigh, then said, "I'm sorry. I don't mean to be such a curmudgeon. I'm just fed up this morning. We don't have—"

"*That big of a budget*, I know."

"Well, it's true. I don't have the money to send my men— sorry, my *officers*—out on stupid cases like this." Dagda shrugged. "I have no clue what the hell's going on. Maybe everybody just woke up on the wrong side of the bed."

"People be crazy, for sure." I motioned to the door. "Come on, let's get back out front."

As we headed through the door I saw that a spate of customers had come in. Jillian was watching behind the counter for me. I turned back to Dagda.

"So, are you going to go talk to Granny?"

He gave me a nod. "Yeah, after I finish up for the day. I

won't take up any more of your time. I can see you're busy. But if you think of anything that might account for this, give me a phone call." At that moment his beeper went off and he pulled out his phone. A frustrated look swept over his face as he said, "Not another one! All right, I'm headed your way." He shoved his phone in his pocket and, putting his hat back on, said, "Thanks, Marquette. We've got another brawl going on. Honestly, some days it doesn't pay to get out of bed."

I laughed, waiting till he left the store to tell Jillian what had happened.

"Seems like a lot of people are unlucky in love today," she said. "I'd better get back to the café. I'll see you later. Come over for lunch?"

"I'm here all day and can't leave. But if you happen to be free, come back and bring lunch with you. I won't be going anywhere, not till this evening."

She waved, then headed back to her cat café as I turned to tend to the customers.

Promptly at four, Charisma entered the shop. I had been busy all day, barely able to steal twenty minutes to eat lunch. Jillian had brought me a sandwich and a couple cookies, which I was able to scarf down on the fly.

I stood the sign on the counter, along with the bell. It read: READING IN PROGRESS, PLEASE RING BELL FOR SERVICE. Then I led Charisma over to the table in the corner, where I motioned for her to sit down. I lit the candle, infusing a faint vanilla scent into the air. I was always careful with just how strong of incense or scented candles I burned in the shop, given how many people had allergies.

"I want you to hold the cards and think about your question, and then I want you to shuffle them seven times." I handed her the deck and waited.

She did as I asked, then handed the deck back to me. I took it, cut the cards once, and then knocked three times on the back of the deck. "What's your question?"

"Is Jake cheating on me? Why has he been so distant?"

I laid out five cards in a star shape. Then, I added three cards to the side. I frowned as I turned over the first card, then turned over the rest. The cards weren't looking good. It was an odd spread and worried me rather than setting my mind at ease.

I tapped the first card, grimacing. "The core of the issue is the eight of cups, which represents Jake's state of mind. The eight of cups embodies emotional codependency, obsession, and emotional or physical addiction. So he's in a place of hurt right now." I reached for the next card. "The queen of cups— this is the woman foremost in his life right now. What's your astrological sign?"

She stared at the card. "I'm a Taurus. An earth sign."

"I was afraid of that. This card represents a woman, most likely a water sign, who can run the gamut from being loving and gentle to jealous and petty."

"He's seeing somebody else, isn't he?" A note of panic entered her voice.

"I can't be sure yet. The third card represents how he feels about you right now, and that would be the nine of swords. I call this the inner demons card, because it encompasses all those fears inside of us about our lives. This is the card that says 'blow things out of proportion, make a mountain out of a mole hill, expect the worst.' For some reason he's terrified of his relationship with you. That doesn't make sense, given how long you have been together."

"He's been jumping to a lot of conclusions lately. When I ask where he's been, he acts like I'm trying to interrogate him. I feel like I'm walking on eggshells every time we talk."

I knew Charisma. For her to be tiptoeing her way around the relationship meant things were bad. She was up front and open, and this had to be difficult for her. I moved on to the next card—the prince of cups.

"The prince of cups can represent an artist, but it's also the card of fantasy. Of living in a daydream world. Jake's not in the arts, is he?"

She shook her head. "He's actually an insurance agent. While he likes to read and watch movies, there's no inner artist there. If he *is* having problems with addiction, would that play into this?"

"Definitely. Do you think that's the problem?"

"Jake's never smoked," she said, worrying her lip. "He barely drinks, and I don't *think* he's ever done drugs." She paused, then looked me straight in the eyes. "Am I just ignoring the obvious? Am I deliberately overlooking signs that he might be in trouble?"

"I don't know. But I *do* know that you're a smart and observant woman, so if you say this is new behavior, I believe you. I hate to tell you, but the outcome card—the five of cups —isn't hopeful. It's the card of disappointment and betrayal, the card of lost loves and broken dreams."

The look on her face made my heart ache. I hated this kind of reading—but I never lied to my clients. And I was too good with the cards to doubt myself.

"These three cards to the side are advice cards. The magician indicates that you should remain as clearheaded as you can about the subject. It also indicates that it won't do you any good to base your reactions in emotion. Yelling, getting upset, those actions will only make matters worse."

"Got it," she said, looking glum.

"The second card—the high priestess—tells me that you

need to meditate on this, and you need to trust your instincts. Ask for guidance. And the two of wands indicates that you're in a power struggle." I paused, closing my eyes. There was something that needed more explanation. I waited, letting the images form in my mind. After a moment, I said, "The power struggle isn't between you and Jake." I sat back, looking at the reading as a whole.

"All right, here's my assessment. I think perhaps Jake is fixated on someone else, but he's not thinking clearly. I sense that he's being manipulated by something or someone. If this *is* a substance abuse problem, then he's foggy because of the drug. If it's another woman, she's filled him with doubts about his relationship with you. Whatever the case, he's having a problem, and it's not with work. *All* these cards are about emotions."

"Should I directly confront him and ask him if he's seeing someone? Or if he's having problems with alcohol or drugs? Do you think he'd tell me the truth?"

I wanted to say yes, but in my heart I knew the answer was no. "I don't think he'd tell you the truth regardless of which situation it is. He's caught up in something, and I don't feel like he can free himself from it. Do you two live together?"

She shook her head. "No, we each have our own apart-ments." She worried the ring on her finger, turning around and around. It was a beautiful engagement ring, and it almost broke my heart to watch her. "Maybe we should take a break. I don't feel like we're really engaged now. Two weeks ago we were happy as could be. But the past few days things have been rough. It's like they changed overnight."

While I wasn't sure that was the best idea, I thought that —for her sake—Charisma might need a little time to breathe. "Maybe you should give yourself some space. I'm sorry the reading wasn't better."

As I folded up the cards, something sticky felt like it closed over my hand, like a spider web. I grimaced, wiping my hands on my jeans. "I can tell you right now that there's some nasty energy going on. In fact, I'm going to light some sage and cleanse myself. Would you like me to cleanse you, as well?"

Charisma nodded. "Thank you. I can use all the help I can get. I just can't believe this is happening." She stood and allowed me to waft the smoke around her, clearing her aura. "I was so ecstatic when he got down on one knee and proposed. He said he couldn't imagine life without me, but now I wonder if we'll have a life together at all."

I finished with her, then saged myself. "Don't give up hope yet. It could be a temporary setback. And maybe, once you're able to confront what's actually happening, you'll be able to solve it. Just walk softly, and don't get into any arguments with him during the meantime."

Charisma wanted to buy some sage water, along with a few other spell components. I sold her a Peace and Harmony candle, some Heart-Ease oil, and the sage water, as well as the reading. As she tucked them into her tote bag, she waved to me and headed out into the dark evening.

I glanced at the clock. It was five p.m., so I set about replenishing the shelves for the next morning. I fetched the dust mop and made a quick run around the floor, then dusted the shelves. By six, no one else had come in, so I turned the sign to CLOSED and locked the door. After counting the till and locking the day's sales into the safe in the storeroom, I slung my purse over my shoulder and headed out into the wind and rain.

CHAPTER THREE

*G*ranny was holding a meeting with some of her friends. They were on the Chamber of Commerce Events Committee, and they planned the official rituals and parties to celebrate holidays for Terameth Lake. They were planning the annual Yule festival that would take place in December. To give them space, I had promised to go shopping for Thanksgiving, and Verity was meeting me at the supermarket to make the chore bearable.

Verity was a Selkie whom I had met at the lake a few months back. She had jumped in to help us take down a Night Hag who was terrorizing the town and killing people. I had learned a lot about Verity since then. Not only was she fearless, but she was one of the most grounded people I knew. She had a good head on her shoulders and, while she could be a little like a drill sergeant, she was always spot on with her analysis of things.

Granny always hosted Thanksgiving for a houseful, and this year I would be helping her, and my friends Jillian, Colton, and Verity would join us. Granny had also invited

Dagda and his girlfriend, but we weren't sure if they would make it.

As I approached the supermarket, my heart sank. The parking lot was jammed, and droves of people were bustling in and out of the store. Terameth Lake had two shopping markets—one a large chain, and this one—Rosaria's Green Grocers.

I managed to find a parking space that would hold my truck, and slid out of the driver's seat, shivering as the rain and wind swept past. I was wearing a jacket, but the chill bit to the bone. The wind was gusting along at a brisk fifteen miles per hour.

Rainy season lasted from mid-September until around mid-June, and November was known for its windstorms, when the gusts would sweep upward to forty to fifty miles per hour, and the rain would cut like a blade. The first big windstorm of the year would send the leaves off the trees to spiral into the air, whirling around to settle on the ground.

The rain slashed sideways—another factor that surprised anybody new to western Washington. When the wind and rain joined forces, the wind would drive the rain sideways, pelting pedestrians with raindrops so hard that the drops felt like BBs.

I grabbed my hat, an old suede fold-up hat that I had found in a thrift store, and held on for dear life. I had fallen in love with it, but now the wind was trying to steal it from me.

I hustled over to the entrance of the store and, shaking myself like a wet dog, stepped out of the way so the automatic doors could close behind me. The bright lights were blinding after being out in the dark evening, and I stood there a moment, letting myself adjust to the warmth and the light. Putting my purse in the baby seat of the shopping cart, I headed over toward the produce aisle.

As I bagged up apples and oranges, along with a bunch of bananas, I pulled out my phone and brought up my list. It seemed endless, and I dreaded seeing the final bill. It was almost six-thirty, so I headed over to the barista bar and ordered a double-shot mocha while I waited for Verity. As I sat there at one of the tables, my cart beside me, the hustle and bustle of the supermarket made me smile. I liked being around people who were active and engaged in life, and while grocery shopping was no joy, most people I knew actually kind of enjoyed it.

"I'm sorry I'm late!" Verity said, hurrying over, her own cart in hand. "I got stuck at Seventh and Pine behind a fender bender."

"No problem. I barely got started myself. Shall we head to the produce section?"

"Do you mind if I get a mocha first? I can use the jolt."

I waited for Verity to get her mocha and then we headed back to produce, where I tried to decide between four different types of green beans, three types of chard, whether to buy baby carrots or pre-grated carrots. After that, it was an intense moment mulling over the difference between acorn and turban squash.

"So how was your day?" I asked, hefting a large butternut squash into the scale to see how much it weighed.

"Actually, pretty good. We're opening a new exhibit in a couple weeks and I've been setting it up. Unfortunately, one of our interns is a klutz, and this afternoon, he dropped a valuable vase and broke it." She grimaced. "Xavier was so angry, so now Robert's going to be an intern somewhere else."

Verity worked for the Terameth Lake Historical Museum, and Xavier was her supervisor. She loved her work and it afforded her a great deal of knowledge about the surrounding area.

"Having met your boss once, I bet that poor kid was

scared out of his mind. How much was the vase worth, or should I even ask?"

Verity added a bag of avocados to her cart. "It's not exactly the monetary value that's the problem. It's a rare find, one of the only vases we found intact from that dig, and now it's so many pottery shards. So in a sense, it was priceless. We'll put it back together again as best as we can, but we'd never had such a pristine vase before."

"Oh, that poor kid," I said. "I'd hate to be him."

"I know. I felt so sorry for Robert. He was standing there, staring at the mess, and he looked about ready to cry. I think he was more upset about actually destroying the vase than he was about getting fired. If it had been me, I would have given him a second chance and assigned him to something less delicate. But Xavier's so picky, and unforgiving. I tried to talk him into changing his mind, but it was no use. So, how was your day?"

I frowned, staring at the sweet potatoes. "How many do you think I should buy? I have no idea how many people Granny usually has for Thanksgiving and she just told me to buy enough for a crowd."

"Well, they're good food. If you don't eat them at Thanksgiving, you can always eat them later. Is she making a casserole? If so, I'd probably buy six or seven."

I bagged up seven sweet potatoes and put them in the cart. "My day was odd. First, Dagda came in with a big chip on his shoulder. He wanted me to give him some astrological information that I know nothing about. Then I had a tarot reading that left me with a bad taste in my mouth. I feel horrible when I have to give bad news to people."

"What's up with Dagda?" Verity never inquired about the readings I did. She understood the need for confidentiality.

"Apparently by ten this morning the jail was full. It seems like people were having lovers' spats all day long and several of them ended up behind bars." We moved into the dairy aisle. "Anyway, the shop was also busy all day long, which I prefer to days where I sit there waiting for customers. There seems to be a run on love spell components. So much so that you'd think it was Valentine's Day."

"Well, that's all very interesting, though I haven't a clue what to think about it. So, are you ready for your birthday?" Verity asked.

"I suppose. I don't mind turning fifty-three, but this is the first birthday I've spent outside of the agency since I was... well...eighteen. That got me to thinking. I realized that I haven't seen *any* of my old friends from the Crown Magika since I left. Four and a half months and not *one* of them has called."

As I spoke, I realized how depressed that made me feel. "I know we're not supposed to fraternize with people on the outside, but it's not like I'm a stranger. Even the person I thought was my best friend there hasn't dropped me so much as an email."

Verity reached over and wrapped her arm around my shoulder, pulling me close for a hug. That surprised me, given she wasn't much of a touchy-feely person. "I'm sorry. That has to hurt. But we're here, and we're going to have a lot of fun. Jillian's party sounds like a blast, and I'm looking forward to it. And didn't you say you have a date tomorrow night?"

I nodded, trying to pull myself out of the funk I had suddenly slid into. "Colton's taking me out to a movie and to dinner. Honestly, I don't like calling it a date because it doesn't *feel* like one to me. I like him, but I think this is more of a friends thing."

"Really?" Verity gave me a quizzical look. "Do you want it to be more?"

"Everybody keeps asking me that," I said, frowning. "Truth? I don't know. I like Colton, I like him a lot. But I don't know him very well. And I'm not good girlfriend material. My ex—she used to accuse me of being emotionally unavailable and I guess she was right. I kept her at arm's length. She was the only serious relationship I've had and I blew it. As for Colton, I suppose a date is a good way to find out what he's like."

We were staring down at the massive turkeys, wrapped in plastic. They were frozen, but by next Thursday they would thaw out.

"Granny told me to buy a twenty-pound turkey or larger. So, let's see what we have." I sorted through till I found a twenty-four pounder. Taking a deep breath, I hefted it into my cart, grimacing as it made the cart shake when it landed.

"You think that's big enough?" Verity asked, a droll look on her face.

"It better be. Okay, I need some ground beef, a sliced honey-glazed ham, bacon, and Granny asked me to get pork chops. I think I'll pick up a frozen pizza for tonight." I glanced at Verity. "Do you want to come over and watch a movie?"

She considered it, then shook her head. "I need to get my groceries home, and I wanted to do some sketching tonight. But I'll see you Saturday night for your party. It's been fun shopping together. Are you done?"

"Oh hell no, I still have a third of the store to shop through."

"Me too, but I don't have much to get, so I think I'm going to just finish up and take off. It was good to talk." As she pushed her cart away, I waved at her. Sometimes friends could make the most mundane chores seem a lot easier.

As I arrived home, I saw that Dagda's car was parked in the driveway. I let out a sigh. I didn't feel like sparring, but maybe he was here to see Granny about the astrology information. He was sitting on the porch, looking cold, but at least he was protected from the rain and most of the wind. As I got out of the truck, he bounded down the stairs, offering to give me a hand with groceries. My leg was aching and I took him up on it.

"Thanks. I appreciate it. I'm sore today, thanks to the rain and the chill. It seems to have settled into my bones. I never thought I'd be a human weathervane, but here we are."

"You bought out the store," he said, staring at the bags in the back of my truck.

"Well, most of this is for Thanksgiving. Be careful of that bag there," I said, motioning to the bag with the turkey in it. "It's heavier than hell."

He hoisted it with one arm while carrying two other bags in his other hand. I had forgotten he was a bear shifter, and they all had exceptional strength.

Once we got all the groceries inside, he began handing the food to me as I put it away. Midnight and Sunshine jumped up on the counter, washing their paws.

We want you to play with us, Midnight said. *Feather toy! Or red dot toy!*

"I'll play with you in a while. But right now I need to put all this food away. After that, I'll give you your dinner."

"Talking to the kids again?" Dagda asked. He seemed to get a kick out of the fact that I could talk to Midnight and Sunshine the way I did.

"Yep. They want me to play with them. Hey, if you feel up to it, why don't you grab that long feather toy in the corner and give them a good run around the house while I put away the rest of the food?"

"Of course. Whatever you need. When do you think

Granny will get home?" he asked, picking up the three-foot-long feather wand. He began sweeping at around, and both of the kittens immediately responded, bouncing back and forth as they leapt to catch it.

"She was here earlier. Let me text her." I put down the bag of stuffing mix and pulled out my phone. HEY, DAGDA IS HERE AND HE WANTS TO TALK TO YOU. WHEN ARE YOU GETTING HOME?

A moment later, Granny texted me back. I'LL BE HOME IN ABOUT TEN MINUTES. WE WENT OUT FOR PIE AND COFFEE AFTER OUR MEETING. I'M FINISHING UP JUST NOW. WHAT DOES DAGDA WANT?

I THINK HE WANTS SOME SORT OF ASTROLOGICAL INFORMATION. IT'S BEEN A ROUGH DAY AT THE STATION, APPARENTLY.

TELL HIM TO WAIT AND I'LL BE THERE AS SOON AS I CAN.

"Have a seat in the living room. Granny will be home in about ten minutes." While he turned on the television, I finished putting the rest of the food away and, carrying a soda and a bag of potato chips and some cheese dip, I joined him. "Want some chips and dip?"

He stared at the bag of chips. "Is that your dinner?"

"I don't cook, just like *you*. Well, I thought about a frozen pizza but somehow, chips seem easier. I'm just too tired to bother tonight. The store was swarming with customers today, and I had a difficult reading to give someone."

I paused, frowning. I couldn't tell him about Charisma's reading, not in detail, but I could gloss over the identifiable bits. "Say, I had to give some advice today to someone having yet another love-focused problem. She thinks her partner is cheating on her, and frankly, either he is, or he's stumbled into some sort of addiction. Come to think of it, yet another friend broke up with her boyfriend today. I guess something must be in the air."

Dagda frowned. "This is all odd. Does love and the accompanying problems run in cycles? Maybe Granny will have some sort of advice."

I shrugged, shoving a potato chip in my mouth.

"Maybe," I said, focusing on the TV. There was a new reality show on—*Cast A Love Spell*. Eight couples were paired up together without ever meeting before, they were engaged, and they were obligated to live together for two months. At the end of the two months, they'd spend a week apart, then meet at the altar. When the officiant asked them whether they would vow to love, honor, and cherish one another, they made their decision official. I'd seen two seasons and it was train wreck—worthy. I just couldn't look away.

"Geez," Dagda said. "You've got to be kidding me. Would you ever take part in a show like that?" He motioned for me to hand him the potato chips. I did, setting the dip on the table between us.

"No, but then I'm not interested in marriage," I said. "What about you?"

"Are you kidding? What if I ended up paired with someone I couldn't stand? For one thing, spending eight weeks together would be hell. For another, I would feel so bad hurting her feelings that—well…I just don't think I'm the kind of guy they're looking for." He wiped his hands on his jeans. "So no wedding bells for you?"

"Not unless they're ringing for a friend of mine. I'm not marriage material," I said. "What about your girlfriend? Have you popped the question yet?"

"Elaine would like to get married. I know she would," he said, staring at the floor. "We've been together for two years, but I just can't decide if it's right or not."

Two years was a long time for some people. Others? Not so much.

"What's the problem, if I'm not prying too much? Isn't two years long enough to know if you love her?"

"Oh, I love her," he said. "But love and marriage don't always go hand in hand."

I snorted, trying not to choke on my potato chip. "I hope you haven't told *her* that."

"Why? What did I say—" He paused as the door opened and Granny entered the living room. "Hey Granny!"

Granny—she was my goddess-mother, not my grand-mother, and everybody just called her Granny Ledbetter—was carrying a coffee cup. She shrugged out of her coat and then sank into the rocking chair, looking relieved.

"I'm so glad we're done. We hammered out the ritual and festivities, and we'll finish up with the schedule next week so we can get the information out to all the businesses in town. It's colder than a witch's tit out there, and I should know." She shivered, grinning.

Granny was a firecracker, and nobody in town ever corrected her. She was unwaveringly right, and even on the few occasions she wasn't, she was usually closer to the truth than anybody else.

"We're looking at an early snow this year," Dagda said. "The first frost sure came early enough."

"Yes it did," Granny said. "I almost lost my remaining tomatoes to it."

I snorted. "I remember that night." I glanced at Dagda. "When she saw it was freezing she dragged me out of bed at one a.m. and we spent over an hour outside harvesting all of the remaining green tomatoes."

"You haven't complained about the fried green tomatoes, or having home-ripened tomatoes this late in the year." Granny shot me a long look, but she was teasing me. We sparred a lot, but there was only love behind it. In the months between July—since I'd moved in—and now, all my

31

appreciation and fondness for her had come streaming back. As a child, I'd loved her. As an adult, I was rediscovering my admiration for her and it felt good to truly care for someone again.

"Anyway," I continued. "Dagda has some astrological questions for you. Meanwhile, I'm going to go play with Midnight and Sunshine."

As I headed upstairs, Dagda began quizzing Granny on the placement of the planets. I thought about what he said about his girlfriend. By now, I'd met Elaine a couple times and I liked her a lot. But if Dagda thought she'd wait around forever, he had an unpleasant surprise waiting for him. The man better get down on one knee pretty soon, or she'd be off to someone who *would* commit to her, and Dagda would be out a good woman.

CHAPTER FOUR

*M*idnight and Sunshine were waiting for me in my room. I pulled out their favorite long-feather wand and began to shake it for them. As they scampered and jumped for it, I could hear the running commentary between them. They were so fast that it almost scrambled my brain.

Mine! Midnight leapt.

No—mine!

Not yours!

Yes it is!

I've got it!

No you don't! Midnight jumped again, this time knocking Sunshine onto his big fluffy kitty butt. At that point they totally forgot about the feather toy and began wrestling on the floor.

I've got you! Midnight put Sunshine in a headlock.

Think again! Sunshine shoved his paw into Midnight's face, pushing her back. He managed to escape and raced out the door, thundering on the stairs. *You can't catch me!*

Yes I can! And Midnight was off and chasing behind him.

I sat there, staring at the feather wand in my hand. Apparently, I was chopped liver. I tossed the toy on the floor and yawned. It wasn't that late, but the constant stream of customers at the store and the hectic push through the grocery store had worn me out. But I didn't feel like going to sleep yet. I paced around my room, wondering whether I should call someone.

As I put the toy away, it occurred to me that I still hadn't called my brother since I had left the Crown Magika. At some point I probably should.

Billy and I had been close when we were kids, and he'd been a really sweet little boy. He tried to stand up for himself, but I always ended up protecting him. He was sensitive, and I always thought he'd end up an artist. I had punched a number of bullies who looked to beat him up or stuff him in his locker. We had traversed many a hiking trail around here when we lived with Granny.

When I was twelve going on thirteen and Billy was eight, our father had died in front of us. He had been brewing a potion that required belladonna and a poisonous toadstool. Unfortunately, he forgot to wash his hands after working. Whether he was trying to hurry, or something else was on his mind, he just didn't think.

That one mistake proved fatal.

We were gathered around the kitchen table, and Mom handed out sandwiches. Dad picked up his sandwich, took a bite, and I remember—very clearly—he licked his fingers. Ten seconds later, he keeled over. We called the medics. They were experienced with Otherkin and they worked on his heart all the way to the hospital. But by the time the ambulance arrived, his heart had stopped. They couldn't revive him.

My mother went into shock. She had loved him more than she ever loved anyone. She shut down, emotionally. So I ended up taking over care for my brother Billy while our mother sat at the kitchen table all day, drinking white wine.

Later, after she recovered, she told me that she somehow felt wine was better than hard liquor. It made her feel less of an alcoholic. But the fact was, she developed a drinking problem.

I couldn't think of anything else to do, so I wrote to Granny. Granny was the only person I knew that my mother would listen to. And now that our father was dead, all of our lives seemed to be frozen in place.

A week later Granny came down to visit, and within three days, she was packing us up, giving our landlord notice, and we moved to Terameth Lake. Granny and I did all the packing while my mother sat at the table and cried. We were a month behind on rent, so Granny paid it off. The landlady was nice and let us out of our lease because of our loss. Granny packed us all into an RV that she had rented, told the moving men where to take our belongings, and we left the coast of Oregon forever.

For the first few weeks, my mother stayed in her stupor, eating only when Granny set food in front of her. She barely interacted with my brother and me.

But as the weeks wore on, Granny's magic went to work on her. She began to break through her self-imposed isolation. Meanwhile, Granny was caring and loving to my brother and me, and it felt like we actually had a family again. And of course, Dominique was around.

My brother couldn't see or hear her, but I could. I never told Billy about her because something told me that he'd be frustrated and angry if he knew that I could do something he couldn't. Ever since our father had died, Billy had grown withdrawn and sullen. He swore magic was the cause of our father's death and refused to practice.

Within three months, my mother had a new job, and she was starting to laugh again. It would be another six months before she seemed fully back to normal, well—a new normal. Nothing would ever be the same without my father. I'm not sure if she ever let go of her anger. He had been careless, and she blamed him for destroying our lives. But over time, she quit drinking, saved enough to buy a house for us, and she never again left Terameth Lake.

I went on to join the Crown Magika, and Billy went on to become infatuated with money and prestige. He moved to the East Coast, and every time I called him, he acted like I was intruding in his life. I wasn't sure what happened to him, in terms of why he turned into a snide and greedy man when he had been such a sweet little brother, but I knew that our father's death had something to do with it.

Now, I gazed at the phone in my hand, uncertain as to what to do.

You're thinking about Billy again, aren't you? Dominique appeared in the door to my room.

I glanced up at her, nodding. "Yeah, I am. I keep wanting to call him, but I don't know what he'll do or say. If I just let it go, I don't have to face the reality that he might never want to talk to me again."

Do you have any cousins you could talk to about him? Or any other relatives who might be in contact with him?

I thought about it for a moment. My father had disowned his parents and he wouldn't let them into our lives. The only thing he ever said when I asked him why we had never met Grandma and Grandpa was that they didn't like Mother, and he refused to put her through their hostility.

As for my mother's parents, they were also dead. They

had died along with my father's parents in a freak accident. Even though it was hard for my mother to return to Terameth Lake, the familiarity seemed to give her comfort. Add to that Granny's tough but comforting presence, and everything felt safe again. Granny made everything better.

I looked over at Dominique. "I might, but I think I'd better leave it alone for now. I don't want to spoil the evening. There's really nothing he needs to know. Granny informed him long ago when Mother died. The only thing he asked was if there was any inheritance, and when Granny told him that what little there was would be sold and divided between the two of us, he lost interest. I don't think he'd care about my accident unless I died and he was set to inherit my estate." I stood and stretched. "I think I'll take a shower, and then go to bed early."

Dominique waved good night and vanished through the wall. As I stripped, then padded into the shower, I let myself think ahead to the date with Colton. I wasn't sure what to expect, but as I lathered the bath gel over my skin, I realized that a part of me hoped it would lead to something more than just a simple date. Oh yes, one fact I was willing to accept was that Colton was more handsome than most any man I had ever met.

I SLEPT DEAD TO THE WORLD THAT NIGHT, BUT COME morning, I woke to the sound of a commotion downstairs. Midnight and Sunshine were crouched on the bottom of my bed, staring at the door. I launched myself out from under the covers and grabbed my robe. I was wearing a sleep shirt, a pair of bikini briefs, and not much else.

"What's going on?" I asked.

Midnight sidled a glance my way. *I don't know, but somebody down there is angry. And it's not Granny.*

"Stay here, the two of you." I hurried for the door, grabbing a sheathed dagger that I kept on my vanity. I quickly thudded my way down the stairs, hoping that everything was all right. The noise was coming from the kitchen, but I couldn't recognize who was doing the talking. Or yelling, as it was.

I hung a left off the stairs and pushed through the swinging door that led into the kitchen. Glancing around, I looked for who was throwing the temper tantrum.

Granny was sitting at the table, the look on her face priceless. She was about ready to let loose and blow. Standing at the opposite side of the table was a woman I didn't recognize. Whoever she was, she looked madder than a hornets' nest.

"What do you mean, I can't be the hostess? *Nobody* does the job as good as me and you know that! I've been the hostess of the Winter Carnival for the past five years and this is the thanks I get for all my hard work? You're all washed up and you know it, Granny. Your time's done in Terameth Lake and it's time for a new sheriff."

By now she was ranting, her arms flailing wildly in the air. I couldn't quite understand what was going on, but she seemed a card short of a full deck, that was for sure.

Granny continued to stare at her. "Yolanda, stop this right now. You're *not* irreplaceable. Since you've entered one of the contests, you *cannot* be on the committee. It's a conflict of interest. It's not like this is an exhibition! The contests come with a hefty prize, and we can't have any whisperings of impropriety or the committee will be suspect of rigging them."

That did nothing to calm Yolanda. She reached out and swept a jar of home-canned plums off of the table. It smashed on the floor, splattering broken glass and plums everywhere.

"You'll be sorry! That job is mine." And with that, she turned and stomped past me as she headed to the front door.

Just as she crossed my path, I surreptitiously stuck my foot out just enough so that she caught the toe of her stiletto on it and went sprawling on the floor.

"Oh dear, are you all right? That looks like a nasty fall," I said, offering her my hand.

She glared at me from the floor, then scrambled up and tried to dust off her knees. She was wearing a pair of white pants that showed every speck of dirt that they picked up.

"You can go to hell," she said.

"I'll be in line right after you," I quipped as she raced for the front door and slammed it behind her.

I turned to Granny, who was standing there openmouthed.

"Somebody sure pissed in her Cheerios."

Granny stifled a laugh. "Apparently so. Yolanda knows full well that she can't be the carnival's hostess if she's planning to enter any of the contests. We told her that three weeks ago, and then again two weeks ago. Each time we told her, she argued with us, and then flounced out. I suppose she expected that we'd give in, but that's not going to happen." She crossed her arms, leaning back in her chair. "You know that wasn't nice, tripping her like that."

"You think I did it *intentionally*?" I asked, suppressing another grin. "I was just...stretching. Somehow my foot got in her way. Or she got in the way of my foot. Anyway, I'll get the broom and mop. You be careful around that broken glass."

I retrieved the broom and dust pan and mop from the pantry, bringing them back into the kitchen. Granny had spread paper towels over the worst of the mess, and between the two of us we cleaned it up. As I dumped the broken glass and plums into the garbage, I thought about paying Yolanda a visit. But one look at Granny made me think again.

"I know what you're thinking, but don't you dare go chasing her down. She's not one of your vampires. She's an entitled and elitist house frau with too much money and too much time on her hands."

"You mean she's a *Karen*."

"Well, yes, but I have to tell you...I feel bad for all the women named Karen who don't fit the stereotype," Granny said.

"You're right. Okay, I won't go after her. But I don't want you to let her in the house again—" I wet some paper towels and washed up the sticky residue left on the floor.

"That's *my* decision," Granny said, interrupting. "This is my home and I will open the door to whomever I choose. The woman has had a hard life, and now that she's gotten a taste for the finer things, she's trying to make up for lost time. She had a rougher childhood than you did, so cut her a little slack. She hasn't learned how to handle her good fortune yet."

I really didn't want to, but I agreed. "Okay. I promise. I won't chase her down and kick her ass. But I don't promise to be nice to her. And if I see her in the supermarket, and if she's reaching for the last package of sharp cheddar, I'm taking her down!"

Granny laughed. "I think I can live with that. What are your plans for today? Do you have the right outfit for your date tonight?"

As I poured myself a cup of coffee, I thought about her question. I had plenty of outfits—both hot and not—and I really didn't need a new dress. "Yeah, I'm fine. I don't even know what kind of a date it's going to be, so I'll just wear something nice and see where things go."

"Dagda called this morning," Granny said. "He asked if you would drop down to the station later. He said to bring your special investigator's license."

I groaned. "That means he wants me to investigate some-thing for him pro bono. I don't mind, but this is getting ridiculous. Since September he's sent me out to find the Night Hag, I've hunted for intelligent insects he was convinced were spying on us, and I've interviewed a woman who hates him so much that he didn't dare confront her, because he would never get a clear story from her. And he's had Dominique and me down at the morgue three times."

Granny scratched her head. "I understand, Marquette. But remember: he's still unsure of himself, regardless of what he says. And you told me that you enjoy being active on cases again."

I frowned, scuffing the floor. "Well, yeah. But...it just feels odd. Anyway, I was planning to chill out and work out in the garden today. It's time to turn over all the plants for the winter, except for your cold crops." I pulled my hair back into a long ponytail. Even though I was fifty-two, my hair remained as blond as the day I was born, with just a few signs of gray in the mix. Though I kept it layered, my hair was down to my ass, and I usually wore it in braids, ponytails, or twisted up in chignons.

Granny snapped her fingers and I looked over at her. "Marquette, the garden can wait. Go find out what Dagda wants. You know he wouldn't ask you if he didn't need the assistance."

Reluctantly, I agreed. Dagda wouldn't ask for help unless he was desperate. We clashed, but in the end, he was a decent guy and he was trying to do the right thing.

"All right, I'll go. But I'm not going before breakfast." I glanced around. "What have we got to eat?"

"You mean what did I make?" Granny asked, a smile on her face. "How do hotcakes and sausages sound? I also made fruit salad and I can scramble up some eggs, or an omelet if you prefer."

"Oh, three scrambled eggs would be fine."

And with that, Granny set to scrambling my eggs while I reluctantly texted Dagda and told him I would be there as soon as I finished breakfast. The day had definitely started with a bang, all right.

CHAPTER FIVE

I had to scrape the frost off my windshield. We were having an early cold snap, and while it wasn't raining, the thermometer read a chilly twenty-nine degrees.

As I let the truck warm up, I turned on the radio and tuned into the local news. Terameth Lake was small enough to be off the beaten track, but it still had a local radio station that handled news from around the area. I was just in time to hear the last song on Joon's Golden Oldies. Joon—a throwback to the 1980s—played hits from the 1980s through the 2010s. She also hosted a New Year's Eve countdown she called "Joon's 100 Most Memorable."

Beck's "Cellphone's Dead" was just finishing up. I loved music, and it occurred to me that I hadn't been out dancing since before my accident. I missed it—my body missed moving to the rhythm. I used to go clubbing when I was an agent. A group of us would go to one of the clubs run by the Crown Magika, and we'd spend half the night swaying to the beat, under a sparkling retro disco ball. I also used to dance all over my apartment. Nostalgia hit, and I made a mental note to see if Chaz offered dance classes at the gym.

"In local news, it seems that Terameth Lake is undergoing a spate of anti–Valentine's Day assaults. Yesterday, chief of police Dagda Bruin logged eighteen altercations, all relating to what can only be termed 'lovers' quarrels.'

"Councilman Ryan Lyon was among those arrested for assault. It seems that our fair councilman has been having an affair with a local woman and her husband found out about it. Willard Brassett burst in on a council meeting yesterday at four p.m., where he proceeded to drag Councilman Lyon out of his seat and attack him. The councilman sustained a broken nose and a black eye before other members of the council could pull them apart. Chief Bruin asks that people calm down, and think twice before acting on impulse."

I clutched my steering wheel, glancing at the radio in horror. Dagda was right. Something was up. Eighteen calls in *one day*, all centering on lovers' quarrels? It didn't make sense, at least for Terameth Lake. At best, the chief usually fielded a few drunks, an occasional brawl, and sometimes a murder case, or other serious infractions. But I had been around town long enough to know that this was out of the ordinary.

"In other news, residents who live near Hell's Thicket are advised to be on their guard. There have been signs that another creature has arrived through the portal. Whatever it is, it's attacking small animals, leaving deep scratch marks on trees and buildings around the area of the thicket. It's also gone after chickens. If anyone sees anything suspicious, they are advised to contact the police. Several large dogs including two rottweilers and a pit bull have been killed. From their injuries, local veterinarians have assured the police that whatever attacked them could easily disembowel a human or an Otherkin. And now, here's Ginny Miles with the social events calendar..."

I turned off the radio, shaking my head. As many oddities as I had seen when I was an agent for the Crown Magika, somehow they had never seemed as odd as the things I'd encountered since I moved back to Terameth Lake.

I had dealt mainly with vampires, but Terameth Lake held dangers of an entirely different sort. While I knew there were vampires here, I hadn't seen any evidence of rogue vampires —the truly dangerous ones—and while I knew the Covenant of Chaos had infiltrated the area, I hadn't seen any evidence of them, either.

Despite the coffee Granny had made, I pulled into an Espresso Shack, one of the best local coffee stands, and ordered a triple-shot pumpkin spice latte. Caffeine jolt in hand, I continued on to the police station.

A PARKING LOT ON HIBISCUS WAY DIVIDED THE LIBRARY and the fire department. Both buildings sat across from City Hall, and next to the City Hall was the police station. The rest of the street was crowded with a stationery store, several boutiques and cafés, a few thrift shops masquerading as antique stores, a bookstore, and a vintage clothing store. The town square itself was about two blocks west.

It was barely nine a.m. and the few pedestrians out and about were on their way to work. Most of the downtown shops in Terameth Lake opened at around ten. Granny would be at Shadow Magic by now. I was actually beginning to enjoy working there, although retail was so far off my prior experience that I was still trying to wrap my head around what I was doing.

The clouds had parted, and blue sky was showing through. But a sharp wind gusted along, and I pulled my leather jacket tighter around me and zipped it up. I was wearing a pair of black jeans and a green turtleneck, along with platform boots. I couldn't wear stilettos anymore, given my knee often gave out from under me due to the injury, but platform shoes seemed to offer extra stability. I pulled a pair of leather gloves out of my pocket and slid them on, thinking that we were going to have a very cold winter indeed. It was a La Niña year, and here in the Pacific Northwest that meant colder and wetter, with more snow than usual.

I glanced up, pausing at the curb as I saw a hawk soaring overhead, gliding in circles. It was on the hunt, that was clear, and I wondered what unlucky mouse was lurking in some alley. As I stood there, staring up, my stomach suddenly lurched and I found myself gazing down, looking at the city streets far below me. I could see a tiny red spot in an alley and my stomach rumbled. *Mouse. Lunch.* The next moment, I broke out of the vision and grabbed hold of the traffic light pole to steady myself.

What the fuck had just happened?

I glanced up at the hawk again. I'd somehow transported to watch through the bird's eyes. That had never happened to me before. But I seemed no worse for the wear, so I filed away the incident. I'd ask the Aseer about it at my appointment come Saturday.

The light turned and I darted across the street, jogging over to the police station. I couldn't run like I used to, but at least I could still manage a short sprint here and there. I'd lost so much over the past eight months. One moment in time could forever change the course of destiny. And that change could be either for good or for ill.

I didn't believe in predestination, but sometimes it did seem that things happened for a reason. And the longer I was in Terameth Lake, the more I had come to believe that maybe—just maybe—my accident had happened for a reason. I just wished that, if it was for the best, I'd find the reason before long. It was hard fighting off the dark blips of depression that threatened to crop up from time to time.

Darting up the steps of the police station—there was a ramp on one side for handicap accessibility—I pushed through the doors. As I entered the station proper, the brick gave way to modern decor. Pale blue walls provided a soothing atmosphere, and the lighting was soft. I headed toward the double doors manned by two guards. They stood on either side of the metal detector. They recognized me and motioned me through.

"Hey Charlie, hi Irene." I waved at them as I strode through the metal detector. Of course, I set it off, but they just re-set it and nodded for me to continue.

I pushed through the double doors. I had been to the station often enough that I was on the automatic pass list. Charlie and Irene murmured quick hellos before the doors closed behind me.

Once past the double doors I took a left, and followed the hall to the first right. There, I pushed through another set of double doors. They were made of bulletproof glass. As they closed, I stopped at the receptionist desk.

"Hey Vanessa, I'm here to see the chief."

She gave me a bright smile, looking more chipper than usual. A quiet woman, Vanessa was fairly young. She manned a series of small monitors that observed various areas of the police department. Vanessa also acted as the dispatcher. She fielded all the calls that came through. We had talked enough that I knew she was married, trying for a baby, and that she loved her job except for stupid people who irritated the hell out of her.

"Sure thing, Marquette. But first, guess what happened!"

By the nature of her smile, I knew. "You're pregnant?"

She nodded. Her smile was so infectious that I couldn't help but smile back. "I found out yesterday. I'm two months pregnant, and everything's fine. I'm so excited—John and I

47

have wanted this for so long. We've been trying for five years and it finally happened."

I also knew that she was a bobcat shifter, and that she and her husband were afraid they'd never get pregnant. I also knew that the bobcat shifter Prides put a high emphasis on family, and no matter what else you accomplished, if you failed to produce heirs, you were considered a failure.

"Congratulations! I'm so happy for you." Giving her a little wave, I passed through the waiting area and then through the office. There were a number of desks but only about half of them were filled. The staff shortage was hurting the department, but there wasn't much they could do about it. The budget didn't stretch. Dagda had made that clear all too many times.

I passed through an archway against the back wall, into a foyer. Dagda's office was on the right, but I stopped at the restroom first. I made sure my hair was still tight in its pony-tail, and checked on my makeup before going to the bath-room and washing my hands. After that, I knocked on the door of Dagda's office and opened it, peeking around the corner.

Dagda looked up from his desk. A tall, sturdy man with short wavy brown hair, he was a bear shifter. That alone had led to several of our arguments. I liked him, in theory, but bear shifters were so methodical they drove me nuts.

"Hey, Granny said you wanted to see me?"

He nodded, motioning for me to sit down. I slid into one of the chairs opposite his desk, crossing my legs.

"Thanks for coming down. Did you bring your license?"

I nodded, holding it up. I wore it on a lanyard around my neck when I was on official business. "This wouldn't have anything to do with Councilman Lyon, would it?"

He arched one eyebrow, and I could tell he was suppressing a grin. "How did you know about that?"

"I heard it on the news on the way here. Seriously, what the hell is going on?"

"I have no clue. And it's bugging the crap out of me. I'm not sure that I trust *you* to interview him, given you aren't always discreet. Heaven knows what you'd ask him. But I do want to ask if you can look around out at Hell's Thicket."

"I heard something about that on the news. Some creature running around? So what do you know?" I was almost relieved. The thought of talking to the councilman didn't sit well with me.

"We have no clue what it is, though I am fairly certain it's not another Night Hag. Whatever it is, it's killed a few dogs, and we're fairly certain it's devoured several cats. The creature also has torn up a car, a back fence, and some barbecue grills. All near the neighborhood that surrounds Hell's Thicket. The claw marks are deep and jagged. So for the sake of the gods, be cautious. This thing could disembowel you with one swipe."

I grimaced. "Well, now it doesn't sound as tempting as interrogating the councilman. Any attacks on people so far?"

Dagda shook his head. "I don't think so, at least we haven't had any reports about it. However, we can't rule out the possibility. It might have killed someone who hasn't been found. I'm not joking—from what I've seen of the claw marks, it could shred you to pieces. The creature actually ripped open the trunk of a sedan. And I'm not talking about just a few slices through the paint job. Whatever this is, its claws can rip up metal."

"Can I take Ricky with me?" At times, Dagda had assigned someone to accompany me. It was usually a cop named Ricky Jean. We got along fairly well.

But this time, Dagda shook his head. "I wish I could, but I have every officer out on patrol today. We're fielding even more calls than yesterday."

"Have you had any thoughts as to why all these fights might be happening?"

"No, not yet. I'm trying to decide what the hell to do. I'm having the water tested, given this is a townwide phenomenon, and I've got a call in to a couple doctors." He handed me a file.

I opened it, only to see a number of photographs that had been printed out. The gashes on the trees and car were deep, all right, and the way they sliced through the metal made me nervous.

"I guess I'll get started then. If you want me to do this alone, it may take some time."

"Take the time you need. There's not much we can do at this point until we find out what it is. Just be careful. The last thing we need is to find you torn up."

"Lovely thought. Got any brain bleach?" I stood, saluting him with the file. "Okay, I'll let you know if I find out anything. I'll take a look out there after I leave here. Do you have the names and addresses of the people who found those marks?"

"Already thought of it. You'll find a list of names and addresses and phone numbers in the file. Hey Marquette," he said, "thank you. Thanks for being here when I need the help. You know I appreciate it."

"Yeah, I know."

As I left the station, it occurred to me I might not want to go out there alone. I ran through the list of people who might be able to go with me. I thought about Verity. But she wouldn't be off work till later this afternoon. Heading back to my car, I ran through other names. Then, it hit me. I knew one other person who would be free at this time—or at least he wouldn't be likely to be locked into other commitments.

I took out my phone, positioned it on the hands-free device, and said, "Jerica, call Colton and put him on speaker."

"Calling Colton now." Jerica's voice was smooth, with a faint British accent. A few seconds later, I heard the phone ringing and after the second ring he picked up.

"Hey Marquette, what's going down? You aren't backing out of our date, are you?"

His husky voice sounded exactly like he looked. He was tall and muscled, with a haircut that was somewhere between an undercut and a pompadour. His dark brown hair matched his eyes, and both his arms were fully tattooed.

"Do you have any free time right now?"

"I'm in the middle of a chapter, but what do you need?" Colton was a writer. He wrote nonfiction, focused on the paranormal. He had first written a book of ghost stories from Washington state, and that book had gone on to be a best-seller. Since then, he had written ten more, focusing on various aspects of haunted houses and haunted estates and the like.

"I need to investigate something for Dagda. I don't really want to go alone and I was wondering if you might go with me? It could be dangerous." I knew *that* would hook him in. Colton was an adrenaline junkie.

"Let me grab my crossbow and dagger and I'll meet you there. What are we looking for?"

"A creature that can claw its way through the side of a car. I don't know what it is. Just something that can disembowel a person, potentially eats cats and dogs, and who can take down a pit bull. Meet me by Hell's Thicket." I waited for it.

"Of course. Where *else* would we go wandering around in the woods?"

"Well, we *could* be headed to Massacre Rock, but…"

"Right. More things in heaven and earth… Okay, I'll meet you there. Give me fifteen minutes." Before I could say anything else, he ended the call.

I turned on the ignition, and pulled out of the parking lot.

As I headed to the north side of town, where Hell's Thicket was, I began to think about the creature. The claws reminded me of the Night Hag, but the MO was vastly different. If we had another Night Hag on our hands, we'd be stacking up the body count already.

Which brought a question to mind: did the creature even pay attention to humans? Did it only go after animals? Or—and we couldn't overlook the possibility—was somebody posing as a creature, getting their kicks from confounding the police?

I reached Hell's Thicket first, so I parked on the side of the road and walked up to the security guards who were manning the entrance. The town had erected an electric fence around the core of Hell's Thicket, where a portal was speculated to be. Security guards manned the main entrance, but it was too expensive to cover the rest of the fence.

The deep core of Hell's Thicket was dangerous. Creatures came through the portal, and few of them were nice. But no one had been able to locate exactly where the portal was, so it stayed hidden, out of reach.

But regardless of the security and the electric fence, kids still did their best to sneak in. It was considered a rite of passage for high school seniors to find their way into the depths of Hell's Thicket, and a number of them managed to spend graduation night running around the woods. A sobering number had ended up hurt—and a few dead—thanks to their stupidity, but nobody ever seemed to be able to convince them that maybe they shouldn't do that. Hell's Thicket wasn't just home to occasional creatures coming through the portal. There were other spirits that resided in the dark forest—ghosts and, from what I understood, ghouls and wights, and other dark nightmares that walked abroad at night.

I waved at the security guards and held up my license.

"The chief's given me permission to go in. I'm waiting on a fellow investigator."

They took a close look at my license and nodded, one of them unlocking the gate.

"Would you like to go in now? Or do you want to wait for the other member of your party?"

"I'll wait. It's safer that way." I paused, then asked, "Have either of you noticed anything different lately? Have the woods been more active?"

The guards gave each other a long look, then shrugged. The first one turned to me. His name tag read BRIAN ALCOTT. "There are a lot of noises from the thicket. We haven't noticed anything trying to come through, though, but most of the fence line is unattended. The electricity is still running, so whatever it is, it hasn't been tampering with the fence. But there are ways to get around the barricades. Most of these trees are so tall you could crawl out on a branch and drop outside of the fence from above. We'd never know anything about it unless somebody pointed it out to us."

The other guard—his tag read DYLAN MERRICK—nodded. "Sometimes I think we're useless. The only thing we actively do is keep people from trying to enter through the gates. Trust me, if somebody wants *into* the core of Hell's Thicket, they're going to find a way."

They were right, and there wasn't much I could say to contradict them. Still, the mayor insisted that they stay, because if Hell's Thicket was left unguarded and some teenager or child was injured, true hell would break loose. At least this way, the mayor could say he was trying.

"Is graduation time the only time the kids dare each other to enter the thicket?" I looked around, wondering where Colton was.

"No, unfortunately not. Homecoming...Samhain...Beltane —all the kids try around then. You'd think they'd wise up, given how many of their buddies have been hurt. There have been more than a dozen deaths in there over the past three decades. But there isn't much we can do. We warn people, we chase them off, and still they won't listen."

At that moment, Colton drove up in his SUV. He hopped out, all six-five of him. Somehow, he managed to unfold from inside that seat. He was wearing a leather jacket and a pair of black jeans, much like I was. I had to admit that I did find him sexy, although the moment he opened his mouth I cringed. It wasn't that he was obnoxious or stupid, but he talked, *incessantly*. And *that* drove me nuts. But still, I had said yes when he asked me out because dinner out sounded nice, and I liked Colton. And while I was perfectly capable of taking care of my own needs sexually, sometimes it was fun to include someone else.

He strode over, and I turned to the guards.

"Okay, we're going in. We have weaponry." I had brought my dagger, and Colton held up his crossbow and patted the dagger that was in a sheath on his belt.

"Good luck," Brian said. He and Dylan opened the gate, and—readying ourselves—Colton and I strode through, into the core of Hell's Thicket.

CHAPTER SIX

*a*s we entered Hell's Thicket, the energy took a peculiar turn. In the core of the woodland, it felt magnified and condensed.

I glanced at Colton. "Do you feel it?"

I moved slowly, trying to keep the noise from my footsteps to a minimum. The last thing we wanted was to alert anything that might be skulking in the area. I really didn't feel like running face first into anything, whether it was the creature we were looking for or something else. Right now, I didn't want to end up embroiled in a fight.

I stopped, surprised at my thoughts. When I was an agent with the Crown Magika, I was always champing at the bit to go out on a case. *I'm getting soft,* I thought. Strangely enough, the thought didn't seem to bother me much. And that it *didn't* bother me was what bothered me. I was changing and I wasn't sure if I liked the new me.

"I feel it," Colton said. "The energy shifted as we walked through the gate. I'm not so sure that it's beneficial for the town council to keep this area enclosed. The electricity running through the fence creates a form of energetic circle

—and that can mimic a magical circle. You know what that means."

"By keeping the energy inside, it can grow. Almost like forming a cone of power." I had to give Colton his due. I wouldn't have thought of that as quickly as he had.

Electricity was connected to magic in that they were both forms of energy and could both be used for good or ill. I had known a number of witches who used Christmas lights to form a magical circle. Not only was it pretty, but it kept the energy enclosed once the circle was cast. Even the low wattage running through the wires created a boundary.

"That's correct. So in effect, by erecting the electric fence, the powers that be have simply increased the energy inside the thicket." He glanced around, closing his eyes as he held out one hand, palm facing forward.

I straightened, keeping watch as he sussed out the energy. The rain had dissipated, but the humidity was cold and damp, and a hint of ozone infused the air.

Really? It's going to snow this early? I glanced up at the sky, suddenly aware of the silver glint on the clouds. Oh yeah, we'd see flakes before evening. Even if it didn't stick, we were going to get snow.

Hell's Thicket was surging with activity, even though most of it went unseen. Bushes rustled, the wind fluttered through the trees sending the last of the leaves whirling to the ground. As the magic of the forest descended around us, small creatures hurried through the undergrowth, trying to find their food before dusk fell and they had to hide for the night. The energy slowly engulfed us, surrounding us in a thick wave as it became apparent that the copse was rife with dark magic.

"There's so much chaos here that I can't get a bead on what we might be looking for. The thicket feeds on itself in order to confuse the unwary." Colton dropped his hand, turning to me. "What does Dagda expect us to do?"

I shrugged. "I'm not sure, to be honest. I think he was hoping that we would just walk through the gates and *bingo*, find whatever it is that's running around tearing up cars and killing animals. What do you think we should do? Should we even bother continuing to look?"

"We might as well have a gander, but I don't want to go too far in. Even during daylight, I don't trust this place. It's like the haunted house that you think is being run for charity, but in reality it's a front for some dark ghostly coven or something."

I sighed, looking around. I had no clue in which direction to go, the energy was so chaotic. So I decided to use a highly technical decision-making method. I held out one arm, finger pointed, and began to turn in place.

"*Eenie, meanie, miney, mo, catch a tiger by his toe. If he hollers, let him go!*" I stopped in place and opened my eyes. Colton let out a burst of laughter. I was facing directly toward the gates leading out.

"Do you think that's a sign?" Colton asked.

I chuckled, grateful for the break in tension. "I have no idea. I don't know what we're doing. Dagda seems to believe that we'll be able to solve his problem, but truthfully, the only thing I can think of to do is wander around until something attacks us. And that isn't exactly my choice for a day o' fun."

"Mine either." He looked around, then grabbed me by the hand. "Come on, let's go this way." He headed right, onto an overgrown trail leading through the debris covering the forest floor.

"Why are we going this way?" I asked, following him.

"It seemed as good as any other," Colton said. He let go of my hand after a moment, and we began walking side by side, keeping an eye out as we penetrated the forest.

About twenty minutes in, surrounded by the cacophony of the forest, I veered off to the right, my attention focused on a double circle of fly agaric. As I paused at the edge of the outer ring, overhead a crow cawed, its call sharp against the soft noises of the woodland. A shiver raced through me, and I heard the faint whisper of *Danger, Danger, Danger* before the bird fell silent. I looked up at the crow and it stared down at me, its eye keen. It took wing and soared down to land near my feet.

I licked my lips, wondering if there was a chance…either way, I had to try. "Crow, can you tell me anything?"

Colton remained silent. I honestly didn't expect anything to happen, but then, the voice echoed through my head, loud enough to shock me.

Danger. Watch out. There's a trap. Don't enter the ring.

I caught a glimpse of fire and soot, the smell of sulfur filling my nose, and a wave of malevolence washed over me so strong that it made me shake. Behind the wave, a low snarl filled the air. I stumbled back from the ring as the crow took wing and flew off.

"We don't want to go——" I started to say, but this time, an audible snarl filled the air and both Colton and I backed up a few steps.

"What's that?" Colton asked, keeping his eyes on the ring.

"I don't know, but I think we'd better get out of here," I said, turning as the snarling grew louder.

"Come on!" Colton grabbed my hand and began to pull me along. The snarling followed us as we raced along the path, leaping over the roots and stones that littered the ground. We had almost made it back to the gate when my knee suddenly folded beneath me and I went down. Colton still had hold of my hand and though I tried to untangle my fingers, I accidentally pulled him down with me. We tumbled into a pile, rolling into the undergrowth.

I grimaced—my knee felt like it was on fire. As I sat up, the snarling grew louder and I looked back down the path.

There, racing along the trail, was a large black dog, its eyes glowing like fire.

"Fuck! *Hellhound*!" I struggled, trying to stand, but immediately, the weight on my knee made me cry out and I dropped again. The creature was almost on top of us, its jaws and terrible teeth snapping. I rolled to avoid being bitten as Colton bolted to his feet.

Grabbing me by the wrist, Colton dragged me up and pushed me behind him, against a nearby tree. I propped myself against the trunk, shaking with pain, as Colton turned back to face the black dog, his hands outstretched.

Shadow, shadow, dark as night
Get thee now out of my sight.
From hell you came, to hell return,
Fire sparkle, fire burn!

As the words poured from his lips, I could feel the wave of magic pouring from his hands toward the hellhound. As the two met—the collision between creature and energy—a massive crack split the air and the hellhound yipped, loud and vicious, then vanished in a puff of smoke. Colton dropped to the ground, groaning.

I wanted to kneel beside him, to make certain he was okay, but I knew I'd never get off the ground on my own. Not without a burly man to help me up. I hobbled over to his side.

Colton let out a long moan, then slowly began to sit up. He leaned forward, his head resting on his knees. I estimated the distance to the gate. While I could possibly manage a one-footed hop that distance on even pavement, it wasn't going to happen in the woods, on a foot trail littered with debris.

"How are you? Are you all right?" I kept a nervous eye

behind us toward the thicket. There was no telling how long the hellhound would be gone, or if it would even possibly return.

"Not really, but I will be." Colton groaned and rolled over on his hands and knees, then pushed himself to his feet. He let out a long sigh. "I feel like I've been hit with a sledgehammer. That's not an easy spell, and I've seldom ever needed to cast it." He glanced at me. "How about you?"

"My knee hurts like hell. We better get out of here before that thing comes back. Do you think that hellhound has been tearing up the cars around town?" I let him wrap his arm around my waist as we hobbled toward the gate.

Dylan raced over to help us, then slammed the gate shut behind us and padlocked it. "What happened? Did you find anything?"

I shook my head. "Yeah. I'm pretty sure it's what's been tearing up the neighborhood. A hellhound, just one of the denizens of Hell's Thicket."

"We sent it back to where it came from, but you should keep an eye out in case it manages to return," Colton said.

"Do you need medical attention?" Brian asked, pulling out his cellphone.

"I should probably see the doctor about my knee, but I don't need the paramedics." I glanced over at Colton. "What about you?"

"I'll be okay. I'll drive you to the doctor."

As I began to hobble toward his car, Colton swept me up in his arms. "It's better if you don't put your weight on your knee."

"What about my truck?" I asked.

"We'll get it in a little bit." He motioned to Brian. "Can we leave Marquette's truck here for now? She shouldn't be driving until she gets her knee looked at."

"Sure. We'll keep an eye on it," Brian said.

As Colton carried me over to his SUV, I felt ridiculous. I'd been injured a number of times during my thirty years with the Crown Magika, but I had never dealt with a chronic condition. Now, my knee went out whenever it decided to. For the first time in my life I felt old. Colton loaded me into the passenger seat and I fastened my seatbelt. As we pulled out of the parking lot, it occurred to me that this was also the first time in my life that I felt vulnerable. And I didn't like that feeling.

LUCKILY, DR. OSTROM HAD AN IMMEDIATE OPENING. I told the nurse what happened and then hung up after she told me to come in.

"I'm sorry this happened," I said to Colton. "I hate that I can't count on my knee. I'm now a liability when it comes to a fight."

"You need to work on that," Colton said, matter-of-factly.

"It's not like I can help it," I said, giving him a sour look.

"I'm not talking about your *knee*. I'm talking about the apology. Your knee problems are a part of your life now, and you shouldn't apologize for them. I can hear it in your voice."

"You can hear what?" I asked, a little peeved. I didn't know why I was irritated, but I also didn't want to talk about it.

Colton swerved to avoid a squirrel on the road. "I can hear that you feel guilty about your knee going out. You don't have to apologize for the fact that you have a chronic condition."

"I don't have a *chronic condition*. I just have a bum knee." The conversation was getting a little too personal. But Colton wouldn't let it drop.

"Your 'bum knee' *is* a chronic condition. It's not going to get any better, is it?"

I worried my lip, not happy about the tears that I could feel welling up behind my eyes. I didn't cry in front of people. It wasn't who I was.

"No. According to the doctor it's not. But doctors can be wrong."

"Yes, they can be wrong. There's always the hope that something will change. But for all intents and purposes, you have a chronically bad knee. Why do you find it so hard to admit?"

I glanced out the window, staring at the scenery. Hell's Thicket was on the outskirts of town, and we were headed toward the other side. We passed through a neighborhood known as Lupine Heights. Wild lupine grew thick around here, and I was actually looking forward to the summer when the tall spiked plants would blossom. It gave the area an alpine feel.

"You have to understand something," I said. "I was in top form for almost my entire life. From the time I could walk, I was a daredevil. My mother used to yell at me for climbing up all the tall trees, and for scurrying up the trellises to the second floor and then climbing on the roof. As a teenager, I was on the track team, and I lifted weights. I trained in several forms of martial arts. Hell, I'm better at parkour—or *was* better—than most of the teenage boys who take it up. I don't get injured, and the few times I do, I heal fast. I just can't imagine myself as...someone with some sort of chronic condition. It takes away from who I am."

I had never uttered the words aloud, because they made it real. But now, hearing them spill out of my mouth like verbal diarrhea, I burst into tears. And that made me even more angry.

"Damn it, I don't cry either."

Colton didn't reach to pat me on the arm or anything like that, for which I was grateful. Instead, he took a long breath and slowly let it out.

"It seems to me that you need to get used to saying it out loud. Millions of people in this world have disabilities, and they live wonderful lives. Do they have special considerations to take into account? Yes. But that doesn't stop them from managing a full life. If you let this limit your vision, then it's not your physical disability that's the real problem."

Sniffling, I wiped my eyes and continued to stare out the window. "How about *you*? Do *you* have any special considerations?" I knew I sounded sarcastic, but I couldn't help it. Colton seemed perfectly able, and it felt condescending for him to lecture me.

In a soft voice, he said, "Not at the moment, but I have a sister who does. And she constantly reminds me that we're all temporarily abled."

I froze. "What's wrong with your sister?" I tried to keep my voice steady.

"My adoptive sister's name is Amelia. She has a condition called EDS. Ehlers-Danlos syndrome. She has joint hypermobility, and her joints dislocate easily. She also has chronic fatigue and digestive problems. Amelia has to be cautious because she can dislocate body parts at the drop of a hat."

"I don't think I've ever heard of EDS," I said.

"She also has another condition that often goes with it called POTS—postural tachycardia syndrome. That has its own *lovely* array of symptoms. When she was a kid she used to get bullied a lot at school because of her disabilities. I spent a lot of time beating up some of the worst offenders. I'm *not* downplaying your condition. I'm just reminding you that there are a lot of people in this world who have just as bad, or worse, disabilities as you. They live their lives to the fullest—whatever the fullest means to them. You had a good run of fifty-two years without problems. Unfortunately, your accident ended that. I know it's difficult but you need to learn how to accept who you are now. Because, Marquette, I think who you are is pretty awesome."

I let out a shaky breath. "Then you don't think that I'm a liability?"

"No, and I want you to stop viewing yourself as such." He exited the road into a mini mall. We were at the doctor's office. "Now, are you going to let me help you inside?"

I drew a shaky breath, then nodded. "Yes, thank you."

THE DOCTOR EXAMINED MY KNEE, AND TOOK AN X-RAY. AS we waited for the results, Colton brought me a triple-shot latte. I thought about what he said, and finally glanced over at him. He was sitting in a chair in the corner.

"Thanks," I said.

"For what?"

"The reality check." I fastened my gaze on his. "In the agency—the Crown Magika—once an agent is permanently hurt, there is just no place for them."

"I thought they offered you a desk job."

I nodded. "They did. But no one ever looks at you the same. That, I might have accepted, except there's an elitist pity that runs through the organization. And I admit, I felt it, too. Oh, if you start out at a desk job, it's different. You *chose* that and it was your path. But among the agents... Well, we were among the best investigators in the world and everything had to be perfect. Anything less led to a quick release. I don't know if I'm describing this very well. Maybe not."

Colton cleared his throat as he leaned back against the wall, resting his hands behind his head. "It sounds like across the agency, *top form* means perfect condition. So what happens when someone ages out of their job? If somebody gets too old to be out in the field?"

I thought about the past thirty years. We had seen our share of retirees go off into the sunset. And it was then that I was struck by how my *own* attitudes had been. "I guess we felt sorry for them. They no longer could serve their purpose there, unless they took a teaching job. And since the teachers mainly interacted with new recruits who hadn't learned the prejudice, they still commanded respect."

"From the new recruits, correct? Not from those of you still on the job?"

I was getting tired of the conversation. Colton was right in his assessment, but I didn't like having my nose rubbed in it. "Can we end this for now? I see your point, but I want to stop talking about it. I feel like you're browbeating me."

"Of course. What would you—" Colton stopped midsentence as the doctor returned.

"Well, you strained your ACL, but it's not torn. You're going to need to wear a knee brace for a while, and take it easy on that leg. I'll have my PA fit you for one in a moment. But Marquette, you have to stop taking chances with your knee. You may be witchblood, but your body can't take a lot of abuse. No jogging. No running. Sprinting once in a while when necessary? A grudging okay. But I'm going to advise you —and I've told you this before—to move into a one-story house. Every time you go up and down the stairs, you put more wear and tear on the knee and one day, it's not going to rebound." He gave me a frustrated look.

I tried to avert my gaze. "Granny lives in a two-story house," I said.

"Either install an elevator, or buy a house. I know you can afford it. And there are a good selection of houses on the market right now. You have to accept that you can't go on as you used to. Next time, you could blow the knee out again and your leg is already a mass of pins and staples. Another operation might not work." He scribbled something on a pad and handed it to me. "Here's a prescription for a mild pain reliever. Take it when you need it. It's not addictive, but it will help. And it's safe for witchblood."

As he left the office, I stared at the paper in my hand. For the first time since I had hurt myself, reality was setting in. This wasn't temporary. I wasn't ever going to go back to the Crown Magika. I was here, in Terameth Lake, with a chronic disability and I'd be coping with it for the rest of my life. As grumpy as I was with Colton, he was right. It was time to wrap my head around reality. I just wasn't sure how easy it would be.

CHAPTER SEVEN

*C*olton carried me up the stairs and to the front door. I had draped my arm around his neck, and I felt absolutely out of place, but he acted as though it were the most natural thing in the world. I was quiet, feeling glum over what the doctor had told me. Until today, I had harbored a secret belief—one I wasn't even aware that I had—that somehow, things would magically revert to normal. That my leg would heal without any sign that I'd ever been injured. But today's little excursion had made it abundantly clear that wasn't going to happen, and the doctor's frankness had underscored it.

"The door's locked," Colton said, struggling to turn the knob while continuing to hold me in his arms.

"Set me down on the porch swing and I'll get out my keys."

Granny would still be at work, so of course the door was locked. Even in a small town like Terameth Lake, we locked the doors when we went out and we locked our cars when we parked them. Crime didn't stop because of a smaller popula-

67

tion. Colton eased me onto the porch swing and I found my keys, handing them to him. He unlocked the door.

"Don't leave it open, though—I don't want the kittens getting out," I said. Even though I had warned them that they needed to stay inside for their safety, they were still cats and—familiars or not—had that streak of curiosity all felines shared. I started to stand, but both the pain in my leg and Colton vetoed that idea.

"No, you wait." He closed the door, leaving it ajar enough so we could push it open. Before I could even try a step forward, he once again swept me up. This time, I was able to push the door open when we got there, and close it behind us as he carried me through, into the foyer.

COLTON BROUGHT OUT AN OFFICE CHAIR ON WHEELS FROM Granny's office so that I could stay off my leg as much as possible. When he suggested renting a wheelchair, however, I balked.

"I'll be fine in a day or so. Granny can drive me down to the shop and I think we have a pair of crutches in the shed out back, so I'll be able to work. In fact, I can drive myself if I have the crutches with me."

"You can't haul yourself up into the cab of that big-assed truck you have. You need a little runaround car that you can easily get into and out of." Colton stood. "You have everything you need from upstairs for the time being? I can bring down anything you like, as long as it's not too unwieldy."

"I've already been enough of a bother."

"Nonsense. In fact, is the shed locked? If not, I can go look for the crutches."

I shrugged. "I think it might be, but even if it is, the key's hanging on one of the key hooks near the kitchen door. It's marked."

Before I could say a word, he headed toward the kitchen. Another moment and I heard the door open and close. I puttered around, debating on when to call Granny. She'd be worried and probably want to come home and I didn't want to shortchange the shop. Every penny counted, and though Granny made a decent profit, I knew it wasn't making her rich.

A few minutes later and Colton reappeared, crutches in hand. "I found them," he said, setting them near me. They were metal, with arm braces that helped relieve the pressure on the armpits and wrists.

As he handed them to me, I said, "I suppose this puts a limit on what we can do tonight. I don't foresee bowling in the near future. And I'm not sure how sitting through a movie will work for me."

"We can still go out to dinner. We can go for a drive afterward, if you like." He settled down next to me, his gaze warm. "I don't care what we do, as long as we get a chance to talk."

Bum knee or not, we *did* need to eat and it couldn't hurt to eat together.

"All right. Dress code?"

"I'll make reservations and call you. What's your favorite type of food?" He stood. "And do you want me to help you into another room?"

I shook my head. "The wheels are pretty smooth on this chair. I'll be fine. As to food, I love Italian." I actually couldn't choose a favorite cuisine, so I just said the first thing that sounded good to me.

"Italian it is. I'll pick you up at seven. You should call Dagda and tell him what we found." Colton headed toward the door. "I'll see you tonight," he said as he let himself out.

For a moment I sat there, then gingerly tried to stand up,

YASMINE GALENORN

but my knee protested and I dropped back in the chair. *Crap.*
This time, it wasn't going to be an immediate reset.

I held out the crutches. Colton had dusted them off, and I
realized how grateful I was for his friendship. I would have
been in a real pickle if I hadn't asked him to go with me.
Which reminded me, I needed to call Dagda. As I listened to
the dial tone, it occurred to me that—as nice as the office
chair was—it wasn't going to work long term for what I
needed.

"Hey, Marquette. What's up? Did you find anything?"

"Colton and I went out to Hell's Thicket. And yes, we
found something. I think it's probably what was razing the
neighborhood." I cleared my throat. "We found a hellhound
out there. I think it was just randomly wandering around,
though. Damned thing attacked us and somehow Colton
managed to send it packing. But the energy around the thicket's murky, and it made both of us uneasy."

"Do you think you can go back out there and check again
later? I don't mean tonight, but maybe tomorrow?" Dagda
sounded a little frantic. "I'd just like to know if you really sent
it packing. I don't want to have to worry about another
attack."

I let out a sigh. "I'm sorry, but I can't go looking tomorrow. The day after, either, or this week, I'm guessing."

"Why? Do you have plans?" Dagda sounded disappointed.

I let out a long breath. "The fact is, while we were in
Hell's Thicket, my knee gave out and the doctor gave me
orders to stay off of it for a while." I glumly added, "In fact,
he wants me to buy a one-story house because he says that
every time I take the stairs it puts an added strain on my
knee and one day it may not rebound. I'm sitting at home
right now in our office chair that has wheels, with a pair of
crutches handy, unable to stand up."

Dagda was silent for a moment, then he said, "I'm so

sorry, Marquette. I didn't realize that your knee was so problematic. I mean, you told me about it but I thought you had healed up for the most part." Even through his condolences, I could hear his frustration. I knew it wasn't aimed at me, but at the situation, so I ignored it.

"Actually, I think *I've* been ignoring how badly I was hurt. I haven't wanted to admit it. But it looks like one way or another, I'm going to be stuck with a bum knee the rest of my life." Choking back my pity party, I said, "In fact, the doctor considers me disabled. This is all so much to take in."

"Didn't they tell you this when you were in the hospital at the agency?" Dagda sounded surprised.

I snorted. "To be honest, they probably did. In fact, when I think back, I'm pretty sure that I've had this conversation before. But I was so upset and in so much pain, and they had me doped up on drugs that I don't think everything fully registered. I don't think I wanted to believe it, if I'm honest. I was so desperate to believe that one day, I'd wake up and everything would be back to normal."

"That's normal, Marquette. It just means you're as human —well, you know what I mean—as the rest of us."

"I suppose. I mean, I knew I could never rejoin the Crown Magika. They made that clear. But I guess I believed I'd heal up and never run into any major difficulties with my leg again. That sounds stupid, doesn't it?" I stared down at my leg, realizing just how much I had blinded myself to the facts.

After a pause, Dagda said, "You're not stupid. You just didn't want to face the reality that you now have limitations. And it's even harder to accept that they'll never go away. It's so much easier to believe that some miracle, some magic spell, will heal things."

"I don't know if there's a magician strong enough in the world to heal anything as broken as my leg was. The bones were shattered. They're held together with pins and staples, I'm told, and if you look at the X-rays, you'll see a dozen fracture points."

"You were pretty smashed up, weren't you?"

"Yeah, and I feel like an idiot." I paused. "I know you say I'm not stupid. But as much as I realize that people don't like facing reality, I never thought of myself as one of them. I always felt like I was a realist in a world filled with dreams and nightmares. I never once thought that I was fooling myself." I was on the verge of tears, but I wasn't about to cry in front of Dagda—whether it was on the phone or in person.

"Marquette, you can be the strongest realist in the world and still get lost when it comes to something that's so important to you. Don't worry about going out to the thicket. Now that I know there was a hellhound out there, at least I know what to look for should it return. You said the energy was thick?"

"There's so much magic trapped inside that fence that it's frightening. That reminds me, Colton and I were discussing a theory you might want to bring to the attention of the town council." I told him our idea about how the electric fence was condensing the energy. "Basically, it's amping up everything, as though it's surrounded by a ring of quartz."

He was silent for a moment, then said, "I'll take that up with the mayor. While I don't know much about magic, I know that both you and Colton do, and I'm sure that never occurred to the mayor."

"Is the mayor human?" I asked.

"No, I don't think so. At first I thought he was a shifter of some sort, but lately I'm not so sure. I've heard vague rumors that he might be a vampire, but he's been seen during the day, which puts an end to that theory."

I laughed. "Maybe they say he's a vampire because he

sucks all the energy out of the room. I don't know. But still, if you could tell him our theory, I'd appreciate it."

"My pleasure. Oh, by the way, we've had four more cases of lovelorn brawls. I have no clue what's happening, but the jail's full with the worst of them and I'm reduced to handing out tickets."

A thought crossed my mind, but I didn't want to say anything before I could check it out. "Okay, I'll talk to you later." I set down my phone, thinking over what had just occurred to me. I'd need the sales books from the shop for the past week or so to check on my theory, but they shouldn't be hard to get. I'd just have to call Granny to bring them home with her.

As I used my crutches to push my chair through the doors into the kitchen, I let out a relieved sigh. At least the door-ways were wide enough for a wheeled vehicle to come through, and Granny had a love for office chairs that rolled.

Twenty minutes later, I was in the kitchen trying to make myself a ham sandwich while I balanced on the crutches when Granny burst in on me. She took one look at me, marched over and took the knife and mayonnaise from my hands, and pointed to the office chair.

"Sit your ass down. I'll make this for you." As she turned back to the counter, I sat down as ordered and rolled over next to her.

"How did you know—" I started to say.

"Dagda called me. He called me about ten minutes *after* Colton called me. I noticed that in the time it took me to lock up and drive home, *you* still didn't bother to call me. I'd better hear a good explanation as to why."

As she spread mayo and mustard on the bread, then

added ham and cheese, I tried to think of something that would appease her. But I knew nothing would, and gave it up.

"Truth is, I knew you would close the shop and come home, and I didn't want you to do that. You've had to close up early several times since July since I came here. I didn't want another instance of you losing money because of me." While she was finishing up my sandwich I rolled myself over to the kitchen pantry for a bag of potato chips, which I brought back to the counter. "I'm so sorry. I didn't plan on this happening."

"Of course you didn't plan it, doofus." She paused, staring at the knife in her hand. After a moment she slapped the top piece of bread on my sandwich, cut it diagonally, and set it on a plate. She carried it over to the table, where she pulled out two of the chairs so I could sit there with the office chair. After that, Granny opened a bottle of sparkling water and set it beside my plate. "Eat your sandwich before filling up on the chips," she said.

I took a bite of my sandwich. I wasn't sure what she did to it, but her food always tasted better than mine, even if it was something as easy as a sandwich.

"Colton and I went out looking for one of Dagda's creatures today. Unfortunately, we found it. Or at least we found a hellhound. I think it's the creature Dagda's looking for. It went after us. Colton sent it back to where it came from, but we don't know if he managed to permanently dispel it. At least it's gone for now."

"It won't be permanent, not in Hell's Thicket. Good job, but what happened to your ankle? Did the hellhound bite you? Colton said you went to the doctor? Is it infected?" Granny poured herself a glass of cream soda.

"It wasn't my ankle. My knee gave out on me." I knew I'd have to tell her sooner or later, so I broke down and confessed. "The doctor told me I have to stay off of my knee as much as possible. He said that if I don't, I may never heal up enough to keep from hurting myself over and over. In fact, he wants me to find myself a one-story house."

She set the glass down, slowly sinking into the chair opposite me. "He thinks you should move?"

I nodded, heeding the expression on her face. She looked so disappointed.

"He said that the more I go up and down the stairs, the worse off I'm going to be. Apparently, every single stair wears down my knee. In fact, he made me face the fact that I'm permanently disabled," I said. "I don't know what to do. If he's right, then it means I'm going to have to make some more adjustments in my life." I glanced up at her. "I don't want to move. I like living with you. But I guess I have to face reality and the sooner the better."

"I understand. And don't you worry about me. I'm going to miss you terribly if you move, but I want you to be healthy. And if my home impedes your welfare, you can't live here. You need to live in a house that accommodates all your needs." She stared at me over the top of her glass. "I knew it had to end sometime. And Marquette, I knew that your knee was bothering you more than you let on. I guess I was hoping for a miracle, too."

We sat there, in silence. Eventually, Granny stood and brought over a handful of cookies, handing me three. "When will you start looking?"

I hadn't expected a huge fight from her, but neither had I expected a quick goodbye and out the door.

"You seem awfully eager to get rid of me," I said, feeling stung. "I know I'm not easy to live with but—"

"Oh, just you hush. You know that's not the case. You're just stinging from everything that went on this morning. You're far easier to live with than you give yourself credit for. So I don't want to hear any more about that. If the doctor says it's good for you, I suppose we have to listen to him. I won't have you put yourself in any danger."

"Well, I guess that settles that." I finished my cookies. "I don't suppose you have any interest in moving? I like having you as a roommate."

She shook her head, a sad smile on her face. "Maybe one day, when these old bones can't haul themselves up to the second story. This house was given to me as a gift, and the day I leave it I will feel like I'm leaving a friend behind. However, on a potentially *good* piece of news, I noticed there are a couple houses down the street for sale. One of them is a single-story ranch. We can go look at it soon."

I hadn't been prepared for that. "That sounds promising. After my date with Colton—we're going to dinner—I'll have to sleep downstairs tonight. I need to crash on the sofa." I decided to change the subject. I was tired of talking about myself.

"Dagda said that there were four more altercations this morning. A thought occurred to me that I wanted to talk to you about. Do you know if anybody's been playing with love magic lately? I know that there are some spells that can wreak havoc in a relationship, although it's usually only a single couple who's affected. It just made me wonder if we've sold any love potions or spell components for love spells over the past week or so?"

Granny gave me a quizzical look. She leaned back in her chair and crossed her arms over her chest. "You might be on to something," she said. "I'll have to look through the ledger, because it's been so busy that I don't remember right offhand. How far back should I look?"

I thought about what Dagda had told us. "I'd look at least a week, maybe two. Sometimes it takes a while for a spell to take."

"Well, there's no harm in checking. And just because a

spell is crafted to work in a certain way doesn't mean it's not going to backfire. So tell me about the hellhound. How big was it?"

I told her everything that had happened. By the time I finished, Colton was texting me.

CASUAL DRESS. I GOT A RESERVATION AT CANNOLI WEST. I'LL SEE YOU IN A FEW HOURS—A LITTLE BEFORE SEVEN.

"What should I wear on a casual date to Cannoli West?" I asked Granny.

She shrugged. "A nice dress or pantsuit. Nothing too fancy. Flats, because you don't want to turn your ankle. So, you still feel up to going out with Colton?"

"You know I'm not that interested in dating, but I like Colton and we get along well. I see so much potential in him, even though he hasn't told me much about his life. And it's nice to get out with friends now and then," I added.

Granny carried my plate over to the sink. "Well, just make sure that if it's only friendship for you, that you don't encourage him any further. Colton wouldn't hurt a feather on your head, but he's a good-hearted man who doesn't deserve to be encouraged if there's no hope for a future. Just make sure he knows where you stand, and I think you'll be fine."

She brought me down a cobalt blue tunic to wear, with a pair of black leggings. The tunic rode high on my thighs, and was low cut in front, with sheer sleeves.

As I put on my leggings, I stared at the scars on my leg. It was covered with marks from the accident, and once again—I suddenly realized they were here to stay. They were constant reminders of what had happened to me. As I ran my fingers over the rough skin, it occurred to me that they were battle scars. But instead of the young warrior going into battle, I was a battle-scarred veteran, the one sitting by the fire with tales to tell, advice to give, and the hunger to return to the field...but not the ability.

I wondered how many agents had left the Crown Magika feeling the same way. How many who had fought for justice had been forced to make new lives for themselves?

But I was tired of feeling sorry for myself, so I shook my head to clear my thoughts, and decided that it was time to face reality. I wasn't marking time like I had convinced myself. I wasn't waiting for something better to come along. *This* was it—my life. For good or ill, Terameth Lake was my home.

I finished dressing and touched up my makeup, weaving my long hair in a high blond braid. As I slid on the flats that Granny had brought down for me, I rolled over to the full-length mirror on the bathroom wall and gazed at myself. I looked good, if a little vulnerable.

"This is who you are, Marquette. Welcome to your new life," I whispered to my reflection.

While I had expected aging to bring its own challenges, by far the biggest challenge was the one in my head—my unwillingness to let go of being who I had been so I could become the person I was growing into.

"What are you thinking about?" Granny asked.

"Not much," I said. "Just...thinking about reality. What's real, what was real, and what no longer exists." I expected her to jump in with her thoughts, but instead she kept silent, gave me a kiss on the top of my head, and helped me adjust the crutches so they fit better.

CHAPTER EIGHT

*T*he restaurant was beautiful, but I had to stop
Colton from carrying me to the door.

"I can walk. I brought the crutches." I held one up and
shook it at him.

He stared at me for a moment, then said, "All right, but if
I see that foot hit the floor, I'm taking over. Other than when
you pause and lightly prop it against the ground."

"Deal." I knew that if I didn't negotiate, we'd be arguing
all night about it. "But don't you have to park the car?"
Cannoli West didn't have valet parking.

Colton motioned to one of the waiters who was stationed
outside the door. The waiter arrived with one of the chairs
from the outdoor tables—which were no longer in use, given
the season—and he sat it under the eaves of the restaurant.
Colton escorted me to the chair.

"Sit here and wait. I won't be but a moment." He hustled
back to the car. He was so burly that it surprised me how fast
he could move. As he sped off toward the side lot, I looked at
the restaurant. It was pretty—the siding was wood, painted a
pale cream, with dark green trim and white lettering. Flower-

boxes lined the windows. This time of year they held an assortment of marigolds and mums. As I leaned in for a closer look, I saw that all the flowers were in pots, fit into holes in the surrounding soil. So that was how they could change out the flowers each season. I'd never thought of that.

"Ready?"

Startled, I looked back to find Colton standing there, waiting. "How'd you get back here so fast?"

"Just because I'm bulky doesn't mean I'm slow," he said with a grin. He helped me stand and the waiter took away the chair. As we headed toward the door, I was grateful that I worked out so much. Crutches were always a pain in the ass, but at least I had the strength to support myself. Colton guided me through the door, into the warm and waiting restaurant, and a blast of aromas hit me—the yeasty scent of fresh bread, the smell of marinara, the tangy aroma of sharp cheese. My stomach rumbled as the waiter led us to a side table near the restroom door. I glanced at Colton.

"So you don't have to go too far," he said.

"Thanks for thinking of that." I slid into my chair and propped my crutches against the wall. As I opened the menu, my stomach rumbled again. Laughing, I tried to relax. "I guess I'm hungrier than I thought—" I paused as the waiter brought over a basket of warm rolls and breadsticks, and asked for our drink order. "I'll have a café mocha," I said. I seldom drank much booze—I never had learned to have a taste for it.

Colton ordered the same.

After the waiter left, I buttered a roll and bit into it. "I guess pain makes me hungry."

Colton nodded. "Yeah, it can do that, all right." He paused, choosing a breadstick. "So, I know we've talked off and on, but you've never told me much about your family."

The obligatory *get-to-know-you* chat, I thought. But Colton was right. We'd chatted off and on since we met in September, but we'd never gone into depth.

"My mother and father are dead. My father died when I was around twelve. My mother died while I was working with the Crown Magika. My brother lives on the East Coast. He's turned his back on our line, and is focused on making as much money as he can. Why, I'm not sure. I don't even know if he has a goal in mind like paying off a house, or providing for his future. I don't think he's married. We don't talk much," I added. "Granny's my goddess-mother. I think I have a handful of cousins in Oregon and California, but my mother and father never paid much attention to background. I lost my grandparents when I was young, on both sides. In fact, they died in the same accident. Both sets decided to go on a cruise and the boat sank. Out of eight hundred passengers and crew, only a hundred and twenty survived."

Colton let out a low whistle. "Well, that stinks. So you're basically alone in the world?"

"Except for Granny. She's my touchstone. Because I worked for the Crown Magika for thirty years, I didn't make any friends on the outside. Those I did make—on the inside of the agency—haven't kept in touch. It's kind of a given that once you leave, you might as well have died." Even as the words came out, they sounded sad and pathetic to me. "I guess I really don't have anybody to talk to from my past, except...Granny."

Colton hesitated, and I could tell he was reading the room. He changed the subject. "I come from a small family, too. My adoptive parents live here in Terameth Lake, and their daughter Amelia still lives with them. But my birth mother lives here, too. I only met her recently."

"Really?" I asked.

"Yeah, she and her husband moved here a few years ago, and we had no clue we were living in the same town until I started searching for her. When I met her, I found out that I have two half-sisters. One of them—Nena—lives in California. She's a marine biologist. The other lives in Moonshadow Bay. She's made herself a comfortable life there...married to a lovely woman, a bear shifter named Meagan. Ari's a hair stylist and owns her own business. I have talked with both over the phone, but we haven't met in person yet." He stopped as the waiter brought our café mochas.

"Are you ready to order?"

I glanced back at the menu, then said, "I'll have the fettuccine with the Bolognese sauce, a side salad, and for my appetizer, the fried calamari."

Colton ordered the fettuccine Alfredo, along with an appetizer of shrimp scampi. The waiter refilled the bread basket and then left.

"That must have been a surprise, finding out you've been living in the same town as your mother." I topped my bread with the herbed olive oil spread.

"It wasn't what I expected," he said.

We continued to chat about family and work.

Colton had worked with the Department of Natural Resources before quitting to write full time. He had worked up in Mount Rainier National Park during spring, summer, and autumn, keeping an eye on the streams. Dagda called him an eco-nut, and in some ways he was, but he wasn't a radical about it. He just cared about the Earth and what was happening to it.

As the waiter brought our appetizers, the evening felt like it was slipping into more of a comfortable pattern. I discovered that Colton had an intense dislike for anything pickled, and he volunteered at the Terameth Lake Youth Center—a place for teens who didn't have much of a family life. It wasn't exactly like the Big Brother/Big Sister program, but had the same feel. Adults—all properly vetted—taught classes there for troubled teens, and acted as mentors.

Impressed that he cared so much about so many things, I found myself really falling in like with him. I also realized that I was quickly coming to realize he wasn't relationship material, and I liked him too much to make him a boy toy. *Man* toy? Anyway, I wasn't going to turn this into a fuck-buddy situation. Colton deserved more than that.

By the time we finished our dinner, I knew that I wanted him in my life, but as a good friend. And I had to tell him that.

"Listen, Colton, I've enjoyed getting to know you so much. You're a great guy, and I hope we have a long friend-ship..." I hesitated. I wouldn't bother using the *It's me, not you* speech, even though that was true. It was inane and never helped matters.

"I think I can see where this is going," he said, looking sad. "I'm not your type?"

I wanted to make sure he knew exactly where I stood.

"If I felt like dating anybody right now, trust me, you'd be at the top of the list. I like you—a lot. I think our friendship's just getting started. But I'm not a relationship woman—I don't harbor any desire to get married. I'm past wanting chil-dren, even though our kind can safely get pregnant far longer than humans. I just... I'm a loner, I guess. And I like you too much to turn you into a..."

"Friend with benefits?" he asked, a sparkle in his eye. "Because if you want to go that route, well...I'm open to it."

I assessed his energy. He thought he meant it—that much I could tell. But Colton could fall easily. He would fall for me, because he was looking for a partner and he didn't even realize it.

"As tempting as that sounds, I think that we're better off

as friends—" I paused as loud voices from a nearby table interrupted us.

As I turned, I saw that a couple two tables over were in the middle of a heated argument. Colton scowled at them, but the next moment—as if totally unconcerned they were causing a scene—the woman picked up her glass and threw water in the man's face, totally soaking him.

He responded by flinging his plate of spaghetti her way, splattering her with sauce and noodles.

She jumped up. "You asshole! I can't believe you did that!" Angry Girl promptly picked up the bowl of bread and began hurling breadsticks his way, one at a time. "You are such a jerk! Fucking cheater!"

"I did not cheat on you, but I *know* you're cheating on me!" Lover Boy decided to jerk the tablecloth out from under everything, but he wasn't a seasoned illusionist and the magic act fell flat, along with all the dishes. The china hit the floor and shattered, shards scattering every which way. Angry Girl climbed atop the table, lunging at Lover Boy. She managed to fling her arms around his neck and promptly fell off the table, taking him down with her. The table tipped over amidst their fight.

As she pulled his hair, slapping him on the cheek, he grappled with her, trying to throw her off. The waiters looked too terrified to intervene. Diners were scrambling out of the way.

Colton raced over, grabbing Angry Girl around the waist as he tried to pull her off of Lover Boy, but Lover Boy leapt up and belted Colton in the eye. Colton let go of both of them, stumbling back, as the cops raced into the dining room and took over.

I tried to stand, but the pain in my knee made me sit again. As Colton returned to his seat, I waved to one of the waiters. "An ice pack for him, if you've got it, please?"

The waiter nodded, still struck silent by the fiasco, and darted off toward the kitchen.

"What the hell—" Colton started to say, but at that moment, Dagda strode in, his ears practically smoking. He stared at the mess on the floor, shaking his head.

"Yo, Dagda," I called out.

Dagda heard me, turning my way. He glanced at Colton and frowned, but made his way over to our table. "Hey Marquette. Colton...you've got the start of one hell of a shiner there," he added, doing a double take at Colton's blackening eye. "What happened?"

"I tried to pull them apart," Colton said. "Big mistake, I'll tell you that."

The waiter appeared with an ice pack and Colton took it, giving the waiter a gracious nod.

"What happened with them?" Dagda asked, jerking a thumb toward Lover Boy and Angry Girl.

"I dunno—they suddenly started arguing, loudly, and accusing each other of cheating. The next thing we knew, they were into a food fight and then she lunged at him and took the table down with her. Colton tried to intervene and the dude punched him." I glanced over at Colton. "How's your eye feel?"

"Well, it's certainly not throbbing with joy, I'll tell you that," he said. "We should just go. We can get dessert elsewhere."

I nodded. I had no desire to stay any longer. "We're going to head out, Dagda, unless you need us." I grabbed my crutches and cautiously used them to stand.

Dagda waved us off. "No, go on." He gave Colton another long look, but then turned back to the couple in question.

Colton carried my purse for me as we headed for the door. I was grateful that he didn't try to carry me—not in front of

Dagda. I knew there was some sort of animosity between the two and I didn't want to fuel it in any way.

As Colton motioned to the waiter, the maître d' hurried over.

"Your dinner is on us. We're so sorry for the display you witnessed." He glanced at Colton's eye, fear on his face evident that he was worried Colton might try to sue him.

"Thank you," Colton said, and we exited the restaurant.

"OH MY GODS, WHAT THE HELL?" I SAID AS COLTON HELPED me to the car. He carried me from just outside the door, as I held my crutches. "You can set me on the bench and I can wait, if you want to bring the car around."

"The car isn't that far off, and you don't weigh that much," he said.

I was muscled and muscle weighed more than fat, but then again, Colton was a big, burly man and didn't seem to be having any problems hefting me around. Once we reached the car, he helped me lean against the hood while he found his keys and opened the passenger door. Then he stowed my crutches in the back and helped me into the seat. I fastened my seatbelt as he fit himself into the driver's seat and started the engine.

"Well, that was…different," I said, breaking into a laugh. "I'm glad we didn't have to pay a charge for the dinner theater." I paused, glancing at Colton's eye. "Well, *you* paid a charge, I guess. That will teach you to get involved in other people's love lives."

He gave me a patient but exasperated look. "Yes ma'am, thank you for the advice, ma'am."

"Seriously, how are you feeling? How bad does that hurt? Granny will have a poultice for your eye—she keeps all sorts of herbal remedies around." I pulled out my phone. "Let me call her so she can have something ready by the time we get back."

"I hate cutting our date short but—it does hurt," he said.

"Hey, we can eat dessert at my place and watch a movie, if you like." I called Granny and told her what happened. "Do you have anything that Colton can put on his eye?"

"Of course. I'll have it ready for when you get home."

As we headed for Granny's house, I mentally assessed the evening. Colton had been fun to hang out with, the food good, the entertainment unexpected. But as far as the date went, I just wasn't feeling it. If anything could have pushed it over the edge, it would have been the black eye he took for trying to help, but even that just led me to feel a friendly concern. I relaxed, and in that moment, in a flash, it dawned on me that I was relieved. I wouldn't have to deal with emotions and feelings and all the confusion that generally surrounds relationships.

"Colton?" I wanted to clear the air, to make certain he wasn't expecting more from me.

"Yeah?" he asked, glancing at me quickly. Colton was a careful driver and I noticed he kept his eyes on the road, which made me feel safe when he drove.

"Are you okay with just being friends?"

"I'll survive," he said, smiling as he navigated the streets. He eased to a stop at a red light and gave me a quick look. "I think you're awesome. But I don't want pity dates."

"I'd love to go out again. Well, to hang out. I like hanging out with you," I said, trying not to make it sound like a sappy second-place medal ceremony.

"I'd like that too. To be honest, as much as I enjoyed the evening, the spark wasn't there for me, either. Getting sucker punched might have had something to do with it, but either way, I think you're right. We're better off as friends." He paused, then—with a devilish smirk—added, "Don't tell Dagda just yet, if he asks. I like goading him."

I snorted. "Deal. Though I have no idea what business it is of his. He's got a girlfriend."

"Yeah, but Elaine will wait a lifetime for a ring, *if* she sticks around. Dagda likes having someone there, but he's always the type who's waiting just in case something better comes around. If he waits too long, she's going to leave him. I don't even think he realizes what he's doing but I'm not about to get into it with him."

Colton eased the car into the driveway at Granny's house and turned off the ignition. "Listen, I knew Dagda back in high school. He was big man on the football team. He had a girlfriend named Chelsey—another bear shifter—and she was on the cheerleading squad. But everybody around the school knew he had his on eye on the queen bee herself—the top of the pyramid. Ainsley Jones was a bobcat shifter. She wouldn't give him the time of day, but he was pining for her. He ignored Chelsey, missed out on dates, and swore she didn't care. It was so obvious that our coach had a talk with him and told him to quit being such a dickhead."

"I take it that the talk went straight over his head?"

"Yeah, it did. Well, junior year in high school, a year into dating Chelsey, she dumped his sorry ass when someone else fell for her and started treating her right. Dagda never expected her to dump him like that, and he was furious, but he realized there wasn't much he could say about it. He never did manage to snag a date with Ainsley." Colton had a huge grin on his face that told me everything I needed to know.

"Let me guess, you were Chelsey's new beau?"

"Right as rain. And the sad thing is, he's never figured it out. I'm not interested in Elaine, but she's going to leave him sooner than later, mark my words." Colton slid out of his seat and came around to pick me up. He handed me my crutches to hold as he carried me up the steps.

"You and Chelsey didn't last?"

"No, we went off to different colleges, but it was a mutual breakup—amicable. She's married to a construction worker and they have three kids. Every now and then they invite me over for dinner and we have a nice evening together, talking. Her kids love me, and her husband and I occasionally work out together in the gym. But Dagda, I don't think she's said more than a handful of words to in the past ten years. He embarrassed her. Bear shifters seldom forget slights. That's one thing to know about their kind."

He started to set me down by the door but Granny opened it before he could and so Colton carried me over to the sofa and gently lowered me to the seat. Granny hustled him into the kitchen where she applied a poultice to his eye, and when they returned, she was carrying a tray with a Dutch apple pie on it, three saucers, and three mugs of hot cocoa.

I flipped through the channels and found a classic movie we all liked—*Men in Black*—and, after telling Granny what had gone down at the restaurant, we settled in to watch the MIB take on the aliens while we finished off the pie and cocoa.

CHAPTER NINE

The next morning, I woke up to Midnight standing on my chest, staring down at me.

Why are you on the long-chair? Why aren't you in bed? What's wrong with your leg? I can feel it hurting. Are you going to be okay?

I groaned, shifting so I could sit up without dumping her off, and as I leaned against the back of the sofa, I eased her onto my lap and began petting her.

"I'm sleeping here because yes, my leg hurts. Remember I told you that I hurt it earlier? Ago-time?" Cats didn't think in terms of days or years. They seemed to think in terms of "ago-time" as in long ago, and "long-time" as in something that had been going on for a while. Then there was "now-time," which included recent events.

Yes, I remember.

"Well, it's never fully healed and it never will. It's a long-time pain and the stairs make it hurt worse. So for now, I am sleeping here." I didn't want to tell her we would probably be moving soon, because cats tended to worry over things that they didn't understand or that they didn't have control over. So I decided to leave that bit of news for later.

Oh. She gazed at me for a moment, then licked my nose. *Breakfast? It's now-time for breakfast.* An excited gleam stole into her eyes. At that moment, Sunshine leapt up to join her.

"Breakfast!" Granny shouted. "Get your furry asses in here."

Both cats perked up. Granny generally fed them in the morning, and they knew the sounds of the can opener, which I could barely hear. To them, it was loud as crickets in a silent room. They bounced off me without any further ado and raced toward the kitchen.

I was wearing a pair of sleep shorts and a cami, and as I sat up and looked outside, I shivered. The rain was coming down, but it was mixed with snow and the chill emanated from outside through the window. I shivered, pulling the covers around my shoulders. Outside, the frozen slush was looking more white than liquid. Snow on my birthday didn't surprise me, but I hoped it would turn completely over to one or another. Slushing wasn't nearly as pretty as snowing.

I needed to go to the bathroom, and while my knee hurt less than the day before, I decided not to take any chances. Granny had left me a couple outfits on the end of the sofa, so I chose one, eased myself onto the rolling office chair, giving myself a good push toward the hall. At the bathroom, it wasn't hard to use the walls and counters to support myself as I headed for the toilet. Once done, I decided that I'd take a shower. For that, I'd need to go to Granny's master bath, given the powder room was a two-piece.

As I emerged from the powder room, I was surprised to see Dominique hovering by my chair. She smiled as I sat down again.

Morning, Marquette. How are you doing?

I shrugged. "I think the knee is better, but I'll have to be cautious on it for a few days." I let out a sigh. "The doctor wants me to move into a one-story house. I don't want to move, but I suppose Granny needs her house back, too. I guess it's time I found a space of my own."

I heard you talking to Granny about it. I'll miss you when you go, but you can always come over to see me, as well as Granny. While she put on a brave air, I could hear a melancholy tone in her voice.

"Do ghosts get sad? Do they miss people if a family moves out of a house, even if the family didn't know they were there?" It was an off-the-cuff question, one I hadn't thought of before. Dominique had been with Granny from the time Granny was young until Granny was in her mid-twenties. Then she had gone on to work for another family but died unexpectedly when she fell out the window and broke her neck. At that point, she had returned to Granny's side and had been following her ever since, looking to take care of her.

Oh, we feel emotion—those of us who were living people. There are spirits who've never been in human or Otherkin form before and we avoid them as much as most of the living do. They're highly unpredictable and some come from the astral plane. But yes, I've known several spirits who live alone in abandoned houses, where the family moved out and no one else bought the house. They're the loneliest of all, I'd say. I'm not talking about some of the more frightening types of the undead.

There were six forms of spirits that were generally acknowledged by spirit shamans—those born to work with the dead. Few witches who could commune with ghosts were born to be spirit shamans, though. They were usually born into a narrow lineage, and they were trained from birth to take their places. The nearest spirit shaman I knew of was named Kerris Fellwater, and she lived over in Whisper Hollow, on the Olympic Peninsula.

The first type of spirit was known as the *Resting*. They existed within the Veil, though they hadn't passed beyond it, and they weren't interested in returning to our realm. The second type was known as the *Mournful* dead, and they were so wrapped up in their grief over dying they seldom bothered the living. The third—the *Wandering Ones*—walked the Earth, no longer tied to any single spot. They generally ignored the living, though there were exceptions.

The fourth type—*Haunts*—were dangerous, and covered a wide variety of spirits. They included the poltergeists and all sorts of ghosts who actively sought to harm the living. The fifth—*Guides*—sought to help the living, and that was the kind of spirit Dominique was. And the sixth type was the most fearsome of all. The *Unliving* weren't the same as vampires—they were corporeal and yes, they *were* dead, but their bodies were powered by will alone. The Unliving were easily able to control the world around them. They hated spirit shamans, they hated the living, and they probably hated vampires, too—though I didn't know that for a fact.

I frowned, dwelling on a question I'd had ever since I returned to live with Granny. "Are there more than six types of dead? I mean, vampires are another form, and they aren't covered under the six types that the spirit shamans talk about."

Dominique followed me as I rolled myself into Granny's room. *Well, yes, there are, but not all of them stem from this world. From your world—the world of the living. Of humans and Otherkin. Spirit shamans know a great deal, but they can't be everywhere and not everybody has the luxury of meeting one after passing over. I've never met a spirit shaman. So, I suppose that there are probably more kinds of ghosts than even they know about. I'm not sure if never-have-been-mortals are included in those six types, either.*

I nodded, deciding to drop the subject. Even though she didn't say so, I could tell I was making Dominique uncomfortable. "I suppose it's the same as for everything—you can't speak for all of your...all of the dead, right?"

Right, she said, looking relieved. *What are your plans for the day—oh, and happy birthday!*

"I didn't realize you knew it was my birthday," I said. "Thanks. Tonight, Verity's throwing a party for me. I hope it goes better than my date last night."

What happened?

I told her what had gone down. "So basically, Colton and I had a good time but I proved my point to myself—I'm not really looking to date. Everything was lovely and the food was good, but given the knock-down drag-out fight, it wasn't the most peaceful of evenings."

Dominique took her leave while I showered and dressed —she was a very solicitous ghost that way, never sticking around to embarrass me while I changed clothes. Not that it would have been all that disconcerting. It wasn't like she was male, and she had been around me since I was young.

Granny had a shower seat in her walk-in shower and I made good use of it. I didn't want to use my crutches in the bathroom. There were too many chances to slip and fall. But the rolling chair fit in there and so I finished my shower, dressed, dried my hair, and then rolled back out to the living room where I found Granny folding up my blankets.

"I can do that while sitting down—" I started to say, but she shooed me off.

"It's your birthday. I'll work the shop today, obviously. I don't want you to chance hurting yourself any further."

I let out a sigh and asked, "Can you get me something from my closet? I have a knee brace there and that should help. It's better than the one the hospital gave me yesterday. I wore it a lot during the healing process." I hated regressing to it, but I'd kept it around, just in case.

After asking me what I wanted to wear to the party, Granny headed upstairs and brought down not only my knee brace, but party clothes, my cosmetics, and several other things I wanted.

"I'll be back in a moment. I have to run out to the shed," she said.

As she disappeared out the door, I headed into the kitchen, only to find that Granny had made me a latte and a plate of waffles, sausage, and eggs. They were at the table, along with a beautifully wrapped package.

I slid into my seat, once again regretting how I was going to have to move. As I opened the card attached to the package, I almost teared up. *I'm so glad you came to stay. I can't imagine life without you here now. We make a good team.*
-Love, Gran

"I love you too," I whispered, realizing just how much she actually had come to mean to me. My heart felt heavy as I opened the box. I didn't want to move. I knew, logically, that I should make my own way, find my own place, but I liked living here. And I'd miss Dominique, too.

The box was light, and small—about the size of a jewelry box. As I lifted the lid, I frowned. Inside was a key. It was old and ornate, made from brass. I held it up, wondering what it could unlock, but there was no explanation.

Waiting for her to return, I doused my waffles in butter and syrup, then bit into one of the sausages. It burst, flooding my mouth with the flavors of oregano and thyme, a hint of brown sugar and faint red pepper flakes. I was finishing off the second link when she returned through the kitchen door, carrying a small box of bottles.

"What have you got there?" I asked. "By the way, thanks for breakfast—it's perfect."

"We're out of salve at the shop. This is ostensibly for chapped hands, but it's also got healing properties that work for those of us with witchblood." She glanced at the box. "I see you found your present—or your first present."

I held up the key. "I did. And...I'm perplexed. What does this unlock? Or is this like a treasure hunt?"

Granny slid the box onto one of the chairs and sat down opposite me. "I've been thinking. You know the guest cottage out back? I've been using it for a greenhouse, mostly."

I nodded. It could be cute, if it were reno'd. It needed a lot of work, though.

"I thought about it last night. I'm going to have a greenhouse added onto the side of the main house here, and I thought we could fix up the guest house. It's a nice cottage—not too cramped, and it's one story, if you get my drift." Her eyes crinkled around the edges as she smiled.

I stared at her. "Won't that cost a fortune?"

"Not really. The bones are good. It needs some patches, a fresh coat of paint, some of the shingles replaced, and a walkway to it from the driveway. I think we can extend the driveway as well, so you can drive right to it. Now—if you'd rather just buy a house, please tell me. But if you want to stay...I rather like having you around."

I stared at the key in the palm of my hand. I didn't need a huge amount of space, and the cats would be fine out in the cottage. The lot was certainly big enough for both places. "I could add on, if I needed to—if you don't mind."

"Of course. We can renovate the bathroom into a luxury spa. So, what do you think?"

I bit my lip. I wasn't used to people caring so much about me. Even when I was young, my mother had done her best but she had never fully recovered from my father's death. And my friendships in the agency had always had an expiration date.

"Thank you," I whispered, closing my hand around the key. "You don't know what this means to me."

"I think I do," Granny said, leaning down to plant a kiss on the top of my head. "I like having you here. We get along. You're family, Marquette."

While I finished my breakfast, we spent the next half

hour planning out what changes to make. As Granny prepared to head down to the shop, she gave me a couple of names and numbers. "Find out if either Tom or Randall can schedule the work soon. In the meantime, we'll switch bedrooms. I'm fine with the stairs for a while, and you can take my bedroom until the cottage is ready. See if they can both schedule times to come out and assess what it will take, and we'll see what their estimates run. Both are good men, but lately it seems like contractors have full slates."

She pulled a container of soup out of the freezer. "Chicken noodle good for you? I figured we'd use up some of the entrees I've frozen since Thanksgiving is coming up and I don't want to take up any more room in the freezer until then."

"That's fine. We have rolls, don't we?" I was still speechless over her gift.

"In the breadbox. Butter's in the butter dish. I'll head out now. Call me if you need anything. Is Verity coming over today?"

"I'm going to call her to ask if she can come help me primp." I paused, frowning. "Her place has so many stairs to the front door. I may ask if we can switch the party to here, tonight. Would that be all right with you? I can clean."

"Of course you can. The place is clean enough, so don't sweat yourself over it. People are coming to see *you*, not how immaculate your house is. Just have her bring all the food over here." Slinging her purse over her shoulder, Granny picked up her tote bag in one hand, and balanced the box of jars in the other. I rolled over to the door and held it open for her, shutting it after she was safely down the back steps. The driveway led back far enough that she could reach her car easily enough from the kitchen door.

As soon as she left, I finished my breakfast, then called Verity. She immediately agreed to shift the party locale, and told me she'd take care of calling everyone. I then put in a call to the two contractors, both of whom were willing to come out on Monday and Tuesday, respectively, to assess what it would cost to fix up the cottage.

Finished with that, I realized that I was bored. Most of my birthdays had been spent working. This was the first year that I was left to my own devices and it felt odd. I rolled into the living room, shifting over to the sofa. As I looked around, I realized Granny was right—there wasn't much to do in order to clean up. Bored, I started to turn on the TV when my phone rang. I glanced at the caller ID—it was Granny.

"Hey, what's up? I got hold of both contractors and Tom's coming out Monday, Randall on Tuesday. Also, Verity's bringing everything over here tonight."

"Good, very good. Hey, I took a look in the sales logs, like you asked me too. Eight days ago, one of our customers bought everything necessary to perform a spell to reveal the truth of a straying lover. It took me awhile to figure out because she bought a lot of other components too, but several of them are specifically used for that spell only, and when I looked at the rest of her purchases, there's nothing else I can figure out that she was casting. That, along with a mirror spell. I'm thinking if she performed both near enough each other, they might have somehow gotten entangled."

I let out a sigh. Mirror spells were used to reflect negative energy on whoever was sending it—also to bounce harmful spells off of oneself. "Would you ever use a mirror spell to reflect a love spell designed to make a lover stray from their partner?"

"You mean, if her partner was led astray, would a mirror spell be a feasible choice for her to use on the 'other' woman? Yes, I can see someone using that, though it wouldn't be what I'd recommend. There's also the question of what combining a mirror spell together with a 'reveal-the-truth' spell might do. I can see it blowing up really fast."

The wheels in my mind were churning. "Do you know how powerful the witch is? Who was it?"

Granny paused, then said, "Amy Farnell. She's from one of the older witchblood families, and she's married to Cranston Jones. Nobody thought any woman would ever tame him enough for marriage. He was considered the catch of the day, if you know what I mean. And as far as I know, he's still a bit of a lech."

I let out a sigh. "So Amy's got fire power behind her magic? So to speak. I'm not talking about actual *fire* magic."

"Amy's always been a dark horse. I'm not sure why, but she never attended the Alpine School," referring to the local school for witches. "She's also got a hair-trigger temper. So, could she have tried to cast a whammy on one of Cranston's mistresses and it backfired?" Granny sounded like she was frowning. "I can imagine her doing that. She's not friendly, and she's too competitive to be polyamorous."

"Not so much backfired, but maybe blew up? If she's got that much energy at her fingertips, and she's got a temper on her, what if she just sent the energy out there in a whirlwind? Should we tell Dagda what we're thinking?"

Granny hesitated. "Not yet. I wouldn't put it past him to accuse Amy before we can prove anything, which might make things worse. We have to figure out what went wrong before we approach her. For one thing, her father—Lemond Farnell —wouldn't hesitate to sue the pants off us for making slanderous accusations if we couldn't prove our case. He's a lawyer."

"So, unless we can nail down proof that something happened as a result of her spells, we don't dare bring her name into it. How do we do that?" I had no clue which direction to go.

"We need to talk to someone with more experience who might be able to sort this out. I'm going to call Rowan Firesong and see if she can come up here. She's far more powerful than most of the witchblood I've ever met. She might be able to come up with a way to figure out how to link all of these altercations Dagda is seeing—"

"Does proximity count? Can't we ask all of the people Dagda's arrested if they've had contact with Amy?" I wasn't sure if that was how it worked, but it made a sort of sense to me.

Granny let out a sigh. "If we start asking questions, it will get back to her and her father will be on our backs. We need to figure out what's going on before we actually confront her."

"So...do you *really* think she might have done this deliberately?" I couldn't imagine someone sending a chaotic spell out into the populace aimed at couples.

"It's possible, but I doubt it," Granny said. "I'm going to call Rowan right now and see if she can come up here today. How's your knee feeling?"

I gently tested it, standing up while lightly bracing on the crutches. My knee felt stronger, though it wasn't back to normal yet. "It's getting better. As much as I hate to admit it, I think the doctor's right. I'm off of stairs for the most part. Thank you so much for the cottage. Call me when you've talked to Rowan."

As I sat back down and turned on the TV, my mind was racing. How could one witch have caused so much havoc? And was Amy even the one at fault? What if there was something else stirring up trouble?

Worrying my lip, I tried to lose myself in the wash of daytime soaps, talk shows, and cooking shows.

CHAPTER TEN

I had managed to sit through two episodes of *Judge Judy* and an episode of *Shift into Darkness*—a new soap opera focused on a family of influential wolf shifters—when Granny called again.

"Rowan's on her way. She'll be at the house by around four p.m. It's quite a ways from Moonshadow Bay," she added. "She has a couple ideas but she doesn't want to discuss them till she gets here. Meanwhile, Verity checked in with me and she's headed over early this afternoon with all the party food and decorations. You'll have to let her in but under no circumstances are you to lift a finger to help her. I told her that and she promised that she wouldn't allow you to so much as decorate one cupcake."

I snorted. "I think decorating cupcakes is beyond my culinary scope, anyway. The best I can do is slap some frosting on them and somehow, I doubt if Verity will stand for something quite so elementary." It didn't really matter to me—as long as it tasted good, I didn't care. On the other hand, it was rather nice to have someone go to special lengths.

"I have customers, so I'd better go. You're okay for now?"

I could hear the sound of people as they entered the shop. "I'm fine. Go take care of them."

As I hung up, I looked around for something to do. I hated feeling laid up—I was used to moving around, to taking care of things. But the house was neat, and there wasn't much to do. Then it occurred to me that tomorrow I'd be seeing the Aseer. Maybe it would be good to meditate. I hadn't done that in a while and that was one practice I wanted to get back into.

I settled myself on the sofa, where Midnight and Sunshine were sleeping, and while I couldn't sit cross-legged, I elevated my feet onto an ottoman, drew a light throw across my shoulders, and found a music station that played binaural beats. I found a song for focus and meditation, and took three deep breaths as I let myself sink into that cushion that trance work brings.

I FOUND MYSELF IN A FIELD. THE MEADOW WAS FILLED with sunflowers—ranging from knee high to over my head in places. The sky was a brilliant blue. To my left, I could see the glimmer of waves, and I realized I was standing on a grassy hill, overlooking the ocean below. To my right, mountains rose, a blur in the distance. And straight ahead, the silhouette of a forest rose, looming dark and shadowed against the cloudless sky.

As I closed my eyes against the warmth of the sun, the pulse of life echoed around me. The bees were active, darting from flower to flower. The quiet rustle of creatures wandering among the tall flower stalks, hidden by the petals that gave them shelter from sight, set up background noise. Butterflies gently coasted on the breeze that was coming in off the water. And from the forest, birds chirped, and I glanced overhead just in time to see two hawks circling, hunting for their lunch.

I inhaled deeply. The warmth soaked into my body, easing the pain in my knee, and I felt like I could lie down and sleep right here. But when I tried, something stopped me—a feeling that I needed to be aware, to be up and moving.

"I want to stay in the field," I said, wanting to just rest and capture the rays.

You mustn't. There are things for you to learn, came a whisper on the wind.

Reluctantly, I looked around, trying to figure out which direction I should go.

You can never go back the way you came, said the whisper.

I turned around to look behind me, but instead of seeing a path, all I could see was a mist that had risen to form a wall. If I tried to go back, I'd be walking into the mist and for some reason, that frightened me.

"All right, I can't turn around. So do I go toward the ocean? Toward the mountains? Or toward the forest?" I could feel a pull from each direction. The water beckoned with her depths, singing siren songs to coax me into joining her at the shore's edge.

But the mountains called too, with their craggy heights. I wanted to climb, to reach the top and see what lie beyond them. And the forest also called, promising secrets hidden among its massive canopy, if I had the courage to enter.

"Which way?" I asked, hoping for some guidance.

But the wind was silent this time.

I moved to the edge of the meadow, where it dipped down, a path appearing that led to the ocean. Even as I did so, a noise to one side alerted me and I whirled, my guard up.

There, I saw an opening appear in the air, as if curtains had drawn back to reveal a secret room. Between the shimmering curtains of light, there was a staircase, made of stone.

And at that exact moment, I knew I needed to follow the stairs. I turned my back on the forest, the sea, and the mountains, and headed to the staircase. Behind the curtains of light, I could see that the stairs were bordered by stone walls, but I couldn't yet see a ceiling.

I reached the opening and glanced back at the other options. They all sang to me, all enticed me to follow their path, but inside I knew with a certainty that I seldom felt that the staircase was meant for me. I had to climb it.

So I entered the opening formed by the curtains and looked up. High above, I could see a cathedral-like ceiling. The staircase was a spiral one, leading up at least five stories. As I set foot on the bottom stair, a noise startled me as the curtains fell closed and the outer world dropped away. Surprised by my lack of fear, I turned back to the staircase and began to climb. I couldn't register any pain in my knee, and—grateful that trance work was mostly done on the astral and not the physical—I continued my way up.

As I ascended the staircase, I strained to hear, trying to determine if anything was following me. I felt almost like I was in a library, given the hushed, sacrosanct feeling. Rustles echoed down the stairs a couple of times, faded footsteps and the soft turning of pages. Once I thought I heard bells ringing out, but when I turned my focus to them, they vanished.

I was nearly to the top of the stairs when I decided to look over the side. Below, the entire stairwell was shrouded in mist. It was the same mist that I had seen behind me in the field—the mist of no-going-back.

And then, there were five more steps to go, and the mist rushed up to dog my heels. My stomach clenched, and I suddenly understood that I was approaching a major crossroads in my life. I hadn't expected it to show up while I was sitting on the sofa, chilling out, but there you go—fate doesn't always play by the time table we expect it to. I was aware of my position in the house, and equally aware that I was actually bilocating into whatever space it was that I had entered. This was no dream or simple visualization. My subconscious had actually stumbled onto a new path and I couldn't stop the process now.

I brought my focus back to the staircase. Five steps to go. Taking a deep breath, I took another step. Four to go. The distant ringing of bells grew louder. The next step and three to go—and the hush of the mist thickened behind me. Another, and I could make out the outline of a figure at the top of the stairs. My heart skipped a beat as I took the next step. One to go, and at the top of the staircase, off to one side, the shrouded figure waited. The energy was purely feminine, strong and steady with a nurturing side. Whoever it was felt familiar, and I cocked my head, wondering if it was someone I already knew.

And then, the last step.

I stepped onto the landing, onto the floor, and the staircase vanished and I was standing in a library. It was private and the room felt old. The walls were covered with shelves to the ceiling, with tall ladders on wheels that rolled around a track that was roomwide, about twenty feet up the walls. On the wall to my right was a window seat against a bay window that jutted out with three sides. The cushion looked comfortable, and I had the sudden desire to grab my e-reader and curl up on it, losing myself in a good book.

The figure was waiting and I turned to her. She was wearing a long cloak that brushed the floor. It was black, with silver embroidery woven into intricate scenes. The hood of the cloak covered half her face, but beneath it, a silvery lace veil flowed beneath the front of the cloak. An intricate knotwork brooch fastened the cloak at her neck. She carried a silver staff with a quartz crystal on the top. As I stared at her, the sense of power increased, growing so thick that I found myself sinking to my good knee at her feet. Everything around me faded away, and all I could see was the dark and luminous figure standing in front of me.

"Who are you?" I whispered, almost afraid to speak.

The figure stood silent for a moment, then she reached up and pushed the hood back. Beneath the hood, the silver veil covered a golden-haired woman with eyes so brilliant that I lost myself in them. They were like twin pools of frozen ice, with stark black pupils in the center. Ringed with a circle of black—with blue flames flickering from the ring—her eyes mesmerized me, her gaze holding me so still I could barely breathe.

"Who am I?" she asked.

I sought for the answer. She felt familiar, though I couldn't place her. But as I locked gazes with her, falling into those eyes, I found myself once again at the moment of the crash. I was flying off the bike, being dragged along the desert floor, and pain shot through every inch of my body as I wondered if these were to be my last moments. And then as I landed so hard that I could hear the bones in my leg shattering, I remembered what I had forgotten.

A woman appeared in front of me. She stood there, looming over me, as silver as the night, as silver as the stars. A web stretched out in back of her and she reached out to one thread, a pair of scissors in her hand. As she gazed down at me, I heard my thoughts.

Not now. Not yet. I'm not ready, am I?

Are you? You have a choice to make, and it will forever change your life. If you're not willing to walk away from what you've been, to become who you need to be, it can all end right here. The choice is yours, but if you choose life—and transformation—I will be your guide and guardian.

And as I lie there, hovering between the worlds, I made my choice. *I choose life. I choose transformation.*

Then find your way back to me. She put away the scissors as everything faded into black. When I woke up in the hospital, all memories of the Lady of Silver were gone, hidden by a cloak of pain and loss.

"You were there," I whispered. "You were there when I crashed. You were about to cut me out of the web."

"It was a time of choice for you. The web stretches everywhere, it binds everything in this universe together, and I am one of its keepers. I am Arianrhod of the Silver Web, I am the Lady of Caer Arianrhod—the keeper of the Starlight Castle. And you are mine."

I gasped. I'd heard of Arianrhod—what member of the witchblood hadn't? Arianrhod was one of the ancient goddesses, and she was a goddess of the Web—of the continuity that bound together everything that existed in our universe. Members of the witchblood community revered her, because she was one of the Webcutters—like the Norns, she could cut the threads of life. Arianrhod could cut people out of the web and send them into the Veil.

"So I could have died that night," I said.

"You almost did. I wasn't sure until your potential future came into view, but *you* had to make the choice. Not me." Arianrhod paused. "Sometimes, we can decide. Other times, when fate has a potential use for you, it's not up to the gods."

I ran through all the things I knew about the gods, then asked, "Am I your priestess?"

She shook her head, and faint silver sparks showered off of her as she did so.

"No, but I am your guardian, and you are to honor me as such. You may be surprised to find your old life not so distanced from your new one, in time. But Marquette, your magic has shifted, and will be more important as you go forward. Listen well to what the Aseer tells you, and follow through. Don't take any spiritual guidance from her for granted. There are reasons she is a voice for the gods." And with that, she leaned down and lifted me up as though I were light as a feather. She placed a kiss on my forehead and I felt the imprint of her lips soak into my skin.

"Glenda. It's like Glenda in *Wizard of Oz*," I said, comparing the feeling to the only thing I could think of.

"Not really...well...in a way. But I am the Witch of the North Star, and my home lies far among the stars, in my Silver Castle. There is no yellow brick road to show you the way, but you will sort it out as time continues. Do not fret about your leg. There are reasons."

Before I could speak, she walked me over to the window and bade me to look out. I found myself staring down at a fall so far and so deep that I couldn't see the end to it. As I turned to ask Arianrhod why I was looking at it, the wall fell away—vanished as though it had never been there—and she gave me a push. I went soaring into the depths, falling in slow motion. Music, like the slow pulse of a low beat, rose up, and then came the plucking of a harp—the strings echoing gently against the sonorous rhythm.

I found myself straightening out, almost floating on the current as I fell in slow motion. I slowed to a feather's fall, drifting on the winds as the snowy depths below drew closer. Right before I was treetop level, I closed my eyes, and when I landed, I opened them and found myself back in my body, sitting on the sofa, with Midnight on one side of me and Sunshine on the other, both pressed against me, purring.

CHAPTER ELEVEN

I stretched, trying to take in everything that had happened during my vision quest. I hadn't expected anything like that. I'd just expected to quietly prepare myself for the Aseer, not have a full-fledged out-of-body experience.

Not sure what to think, still in a haze brought on from meeting Arianrhod, I slowly looked around me. Everything seemed slightly different—and yet it was the same. Midnight and Sunshine stood and stretched, both doing the Halloween-cat pose with the curled tail.

Are you all right? You were a long ways out. Midnight gazed at me. She let out a little squeak.

"Yes, I was. I think I'm fine. Do you know what happened? Do you know who I visited while I was out?" I had no clue how much cats understood about the gods. Hell, I didn't even know how much *I* understood about the gods.

You were with the Lady I've seen by your bedside several times.

I blinked. Say what? I had no clue what she was talking about. If Arianrhod had been at my bedside, I knew nothing about it. I glanced at Sunshine.

"What about you? Have you seen her before?"

Only when you're asleep. She comes to check in on you now and then. She told us not to tell you—that you needed to find out about her by yourself. I guess it's okay now, though, since you saw her. Sunshine yawned again, then curled up by my side. *Nap now?*

"I'm sorry, chickie, but I need to think for a bit, and I'm hungry. Nap later, okay?"

Okay. Sunshine jumped off the sofa and headed for the bathroom, to use the litter box. Midnight stayed behind. She put a paw on my arm, giving me a soulful look.

She is powerful. Listen to what she told you. She walks in frost, and breathes out mist.

That was downright poetic. I hesitated. "Do you think it's safe?"

You know that nothing is fully safe, but she is truthful, and that is more than many beings, be they gods or people or ghosts. Midnight shook her head and scratched behind her ear.

"You realize you seem far more...*human* than a normal cat?" I reached down to stroke her cheek. She rubbed against my hand, purring.

I won't hold that comment against you, even though it's not a compliment. But I understand what you mean. Midnight purped and bounced off the sofa, heading toward the kitchen.

I WAS IN THE MIDDLE OF EATING A HAM SANDWICH AND writing down what had happened when the doorbell rang. As I rolled myself to the door—it was quicker than using the crutches, though my knee was starting to feel a lot more stable—I was still feeling introspective. While I'd heard about the gods for years, and once in a while during a Circle had felt their power, I'd never before encountered one. I knew a lot of the witchblood community worked with the gods, but I'd never had the chance before. I felt honored, humbled, and more than a little afraid.

As I opened the door, Verity was waiting with three shopping bags full of supplies. She gave me a brief hug—she wasn't a hugger and so that was as good as a kiss—and swept past me, bags in hand.

"I can carry one of those," I started to say, but she breezed by me as though they weighed nothing.

"No, you go watch television or something. I promised Granny that I wouldn't put you to work and I intend to stick to my promise. I have two more trips to the car to make, though, so if you wouldn't mind standing watch at the door, I'd appreciate it." She leaned over to boop Midnight on the nose. "You and your brother stay away from the outside, do you hear me?"

Midnight looked both a little indignant and wide-eyed. Verity intimidated everyone. Except Granny, of course, but she impressed Granny and that was close enough.

I looked at Midnight and Sunshine, who were standing near the counter. "Don't even think of trying to help Verity, she'll chase you off the counter. Will you be good and go upstairs to play for a bit?"

Midnight let out a yawn. *I'm tired. Nap time.*

Sunshine blinked. *Me too.*

They loped up the stairs, heading for the spare room that we'd set up for them. While they had the run of the house, if we needed to contain them for some reason, we were able to put them in the guest bedroom and they had a litter box, food and water, toys and the guest bed to sleep on there. They also had a second cat tree next to the window.

Once they were out of sight, Verity darted back to her car and I manned the door, letting her in. The second trip, she carried in two more bags of supplies. The third, she was holding a large cake box. I knew it was cake because it had the Winston's Bakery logo on it. My mouth watered—they had the best baked goods in the state.

I tried to get a peek at what she was doing in the kitchen and dining room, but she chased me out and so I retreated to the living room. Feeling antsy, I went back to my laptop where I finished writing down everything that had happened during my vision. As with dreams, it was fading, but the energy behind it remained.

I paused near the end, those pale frost eyes of hers still burnt into my brain. I had never felt so exposed, so fully seen. But even though the experience had faded a little, the memory of her standing over me during the accident hadn't. She had been there, gazing down at me, and now I couldn't forget it.

I wondered why I had blanked it out. Maybe it was just the pain, or maybe it was the shock? I searched my gut, looking for the reason, but only found silence. The whole accident felt like one massive jigsaw puzzle with several important pieces missing.

A moment later, while I was deep in thought, Verity poked her head through the curtains. "You like red velvet cake, don't you? I asked Granny and she said you did."

I nodded. "Love it. Actually, it's one of my favorites."

"Good—"

Before she could disappear back into the kitchen, I said, "Verity? Can I ask you something?"

"What is it?" She paused, looking at me. She must have noticed something about my expression or felt my concern, because she crossed to the recliner, which was opposite me, and sat down. "What's going on?"

I hesitated, then said, "I know you're not witchblood, so this may not fully make sense, but I need to talk about something that happened shortly before you arrived." I told her about the vision, about Arianrhod, and what she had said.

"I've never been focused that much on my magic, so this feels so...out of step for me. I always have focused on my physical strengths. I've had an innate amount of luck hunting down vampires and chaos magicians, and my instincts are good. But after what Arianrhod said, I'm almost afraid to go see the Aseer tomorrow."

Verity digested everything I told her, then asked, "What are you afraid will happen?"

I thought about her question for a moment. What *was* I afraid of? I never flinched when facing new assignments. So why was I uncertain about this? What did I think might happen? Or was it what might *not* happen that made me fear?

Letting out a sigh, I said, "For one thing, what if I suck at this? What if I suck at learning to focus on my magic instead of my body?"

"Then you'll practice like anybody taking a new course. You have the abilities, you just haven't trained them, correct?" Verity was so matter-of-fact that her voice calmed me down.

I nodded. "Yes, that's true. I also...I'm afraid...I felt something so deep and so overwhelming during the experience that...the potential left me overwhelmed. So maybe I'm afraid of what I might be able to do? I saw the web in her hands, Verity. When she was standing beside me at the accident, she was ready to cut me out of this world. I agreed to change, to turn to a new path, in order to stay alive. And now, it's time to pay the piper, so to speak."

Verity leaned back in her chair, crossing her arms. "So you're both afraid of failure and of success? That leaves limbo, my friend. That leaves you stuck in the middle of the river, without a paddle. Only you *do* have the paddle, you're just afraid to use it. You can't run scared, Marquette. You can't wait for something to happen. You're not that type of person."

She was right—I'd never been indecisive in my life before now.

"I like to know where I'm going. I knew when I signed up with the Crown Magika, there would be danger, but I also knew that I was willing to face it. But I had a direction—a path. I was given assignments and I either fulfilled them, or I failed. And I never failed. Not till the last. I accomplished every task I was handed, and everybody saw me as one of the best. Now, I have to start all over."

"*There*—right there. You have to start all over. It doesn't seem fair, does it? Just when you're at the height of your fame, the game changes on you, and you're on a new playing field, with all new rules, new expectations, and you're afraid you won't measure up. So it's easier to refuse to play than possibly find out you're not a master of this game as well. Am I right?" She didn't sound gleeful—she was just stating a fact.

I thought about it for a moment, then nodded. She was right. I was terrified I'd end up looking like an idiot. I was angry that all my accomplishments in the past seemed to add up to zilch. And I was still bitter at the Crown Magika for throwing me away like a used tissue.

Ashamed that I was that shallow, I grimaced. "I hate to admit it, but you're right. If I can't be the best, I don't want to play at all."

"But you can't know how things will go till you try." Verity paused, then added, "No matter what happens, nobody can ever take away what you've already accomplished. You'll always be one of the best agents that the Crown Magika had. You'll always be known for what you've already done."

"I guess I know that," I said. "But what if it's a steady decline from here?"

"That's up to you. Do you really think Arianrhod would bother talking to you if she thought you were on a one-way downhill trip?"

That was a good point, and made me feel better than anything else she could have said. The gods didn't talk to those who weren't important—granted, the importance was firmly within the eyes of the gods, but that itself should be more important than anything else. I realized my ego was in danger of overturning my life. Being cast aside stung, but when I looked at things logically, taking ego out of it, the fact was I would have been a danger back out in the field. With my bum knee, there was no way I could have held up my end of a mission if my leg gave out. And if it was at the wrong time, I could have endangered the lives of others.

"They were right," I said, staring at the words on my laptop screen. "They were right to let me go. And since I couldn't face taking a desk job there, what else could they do? I would have felt horrible if I caused the death of another agent, and that could have happened."

"Knowing what you know now, if you were offered a desk job with them again—right now—what would you say?" Verity certainly knew how to get to the center of the matter.

I looked up and shook my head. "No, I still wouldn't go back. I'd rather be here, helping Granny, helping Dagda. At least I feel like I'm actually doing something important—something that helps people directly."

"You'd be helping in a desk job—" Verity started to say, but I stopped her.

"I know, and I know that every job has its importance, but I wouldn't be using my talents. I wouldn't be happy. I'm not cut out to be a secretary."

"You're not cut out to be an adjunct member of the team. You need to be front and center. There's nothing wrong with that. There are those much better suited for those jobs—their strengths give them a quiet command over keeping things organized. You're a leader, Marquette. You should just acknowledge the fact and quit feeling embarrassed about it.

That's why you felt so angry. They took away your territory. But now you have to mark a new one. Preferably one that utilizes your strengths." She stood, adjusting her apron. "All right, I need to get back to the kitchen, but mark my words, what happened during your vision quest this morning? You'd better explore it. And don't forget to tell the Aseer everything that happened."

As she headed back to the kitchen, I stared at the screen. She was right. What had happened this morning was a gift, and Arianrhod's guidance was an even greater gift. If I didn't give it the credence it deserved, I was a fool.

As I finished typing up my notes, I thought I heard a laugh coming off the wind. It was Arianrhod. She was listening, and if it didn't sound so impertinent, I'd say she was having fun watching me figure out my tangle of emotions.

VERITY HAD FILLED THE DINING ROOM WITH STREAMERS and balloons, and the table was covered with a long fuchsia table runner. Paper plates—sturdy ones—and cups were at one end of the table. I counted three types of salad—potato, macaroni, and green—and a huge basket of rolls sat to one side. A cooler full of soda sat on the floor next to the sideboard, which had the cake on it. Two-tiered, it was frosted with marbled cream cheese icing—pink and white—and I could smell the fragrant scent of red velvet. My mouth watered. Bowls of potato chips, crackers, and dip filled the other side.

"Granny's bringing the fried chicken," Verity said. "And we're having spaghetti with meatballs."

I wanted to dive in immediately, but I knew Verity would slap my hands if I did. So I forced myself back into the living room, deciding I should dress for the party. Granny had brought down my black palazzo pants and gold sequined tank top, as well as a black lace overshirt and ballerina flats. I rolled myself into her bedroom and changed, then fixed my makeup. By the time I was ready, I looked downright festive. As I returned to the living room, Granny arrived home.

"I closed up shop early today," she said. "I brought you something—two things. Outside, you'll find a little rental car that's easy to get into and out of. You can't drive your truck right now. And I also stopped and picked up something that I know you don't want, but it's easier to maneuver than that office chair." She pointed to the wheelchair beside her. It was sleek, looked new, and even though I wanted to protest that I didn't need it, I knew that my leg wasn't fully up to me lurching around on crutches.

"Thanks," I said ruefully, easing myself off the office chair and sitting in the wheelchair. It wasn't quite as cushy as the office chair, but it let me put my leg up, which would help heal the knee faster. "I'll be so glad when I'm back on my feet."

"I will too. I want you feeling better, able to get up and move around. I'll just put this away and then use the restroom." Granny rolled the office chair back to the office as I followed Verity into the kitchen.

The kitchen table was covered with prep work, and with more bread. A huge vat of spaghetti sat in a giant tureen, smelling full of tomatoey goodness. Verity arranged chicken on a huge platter and carried it out to add to the feast. I followed her into the dining room again as the doorbell rang and I maneuvered past her to open the door.

A woman stood there, lean and weathered so that she looked like she belonged in the desert. She had long silver hair, braided and pinned around her head. As she caught sight of me, her eyes danced and she smiled. "You must be Marquette."

I nodded. "Rowan?"

"Yes, Rowan Firesong. Did I interrupt something?" She looked me up and down.

"Not at all. I'm Marquette, Granny's goddess-daughter. Please come in. We're celebrating my birthday and you're quite welcome to stay. Granny will be right out."

I invited her in, and by the time we reached the living room, Granny had returned. She greeted Rowan and motioned for her to take a seat.

"Before anybody else arrives, we should talk. The chief of police will be here tonight and I don't want him to know our thoughts before we've had time to sort matters out. He's... overly quick and jumps to conclusions." Granny motioned to me. "Why don't you tell her what's been going on with Dagda, and then I'll tell her what I found out about Amy."

I laid out everything that Dagda had been facing. "He wants me to research what's going on and help him solve this, but honestly, I'm just as lost as the next person."

Rowan listened closely, and I could feel her curiosity build.

"Tell me what this woman—Amy—bought, again?"

Granny laid out the list of ingredients.

"That's very telling. How experienced would you say she is?" Rowan wasn't taking notes, but I could tell she was mentally filing everything away. I actually felt a little cowed in her presence. She seemed to have everything going on for her, starting from being a fiery, well-shaped middle-aged woman to her innate sense of power. Although Granny had said Rowan was far older than middle-aged, she didn't look it or seem it. But power—power, Rowan had. She tingled, sparks flying off her aura. Her eyes pierced everything she looked at. She smoldered, and I felt like a pale shadow next to her.

"Amy has power behind her, but she's a loose cannon

when it comes to controlling it," Granny said. "She's married to a player, but she's jealous and territorial."

"So you think she might have cast a spell and it went awry?"

I nodded. "Something has to be behind this spate of incidents." I told her about what Colton and I had seen in the restaurant. "One moment they were eating dinner, nice and quiet like the rest of us, and the next moment they were in a knock-down, drag-out food fight that turned physical. They accused each other of cheating."

"I see," Rowan said. "Do you have a private room where I can set up to scry? And...I wish that someone who's been part of this could come in—"

"Jillian!" I said.

"Jillian? Really?" Granny turned to me. "She was arrested?"

"No, but her boyfriend broke up with her. And it sounded suspiciously like the other cases to me. She'll be here soon," I added, turning to Rowan.

"Good. That may help." Rowan followed Granny, who led her into the office.

I turned back to Verity. "I'm glad I'm not involved with anybody right now," I said.

"Speaking of, how did your date with Colton go?"

"Not bad. But I just want to be friends. I feel like I'm somehow abnormal. I don't crave a life partner. I enjoy sex, but I can separate it from emotion. For me, it's just a good time, it doesn't run deeper." I shrugged. "I guess it's just my nature."

"Better you know that upfront rather than trying to force yourself into a mold," Verity said. "Look at me—I'm more asexual. I don't have much interest in sex and I'm well equipped to satisfy my own needs. I prefer the company of trees than the company of men...or women—either way."

I nodded. "I'm bisexual, but I don't want to share my space."

The bell rang, and Verity answered. It was Jillian, followed by Dagda. I left Dagda to Verity and motioned for Jillian to follow me. We entered the office and I introduced her to Rowan, leaving her there so Granny could explain what we needed.

Heading back to the living room, I saw that several others had arrived. Even though I was feeling more introspective than I wanted to admit, I rolled into their midst to celebrate the fact that I was now fifty-three years old.

CHAPTER TWELVE

*T*he party was fun, but I found myself oddly relieved when everybody went home except for Granny, Rowan, Jillian, and me. Verity wanted to stay, but she had an early morning at the museum coming up and had to get home.

As the four of us curled up in the living room, I had a chance to study Rowan. After consulting with Jillian, she had joined the party, talking mostly to Granny. The witchblood in her veins was perhaps the strongest I'd sensed, with the exception of the Aseer, when I was young. Rowan reminded me of a coiled serpent. I wouldn't want to be in her line of attack.

"So, tell me, did you find anything yet?" I was far more curious about what Rowan might have discovered than I was in continuing my birthday celebration. I liked holidays, but if she had discovered something, I wanted to know.

"Actually, yes, I did." Rowan glanced at Granny, who nodded. "What's going on definitely seems to be the result of a spell that backfired, but not quite in the way you might think."

"I feel like Typhoid Mary," Jillian said.

"You are—and so is everybody else who came into contact with Amy in the first few days after she cast the spell." Rowan shrugged. "Not your fault, but you—and everybody else she touched—is contagious now."

"Contagious?" I sat up. "What the hell?"

"The results of the spell backfiring didn't just shoot energy into the air. It created...think of it as a magical virus. And anybody Amy touched during the first few days was infected and can pass it on. I've encountered this a few times before in my life, and it's never easy to deal with the aftermath. You should be grateful that all she was casting was some sort of love spell. If she'd been casting dark magic, as in death magic or hexing magic, people would be *dead* instead of bickering about who's fucking who."

I tried to process what she was saying. "How does one create a magical virus?"

"I believe she was furious when she cast the spell. When working with magic, you always have to watch your emotions, or you risk imposing unwanted influences over the end result. The subconscious is a powerful weapon, especially for witch-blood. Amy was so angry that she actually managed to give life to the spell itself. It took on a form of sentience, and when spells do that, they're usually composed of millions of tiny energy fragments that form a hive mind. In this case, the hive mind's focus was infused with the belief that partners cheat, and that confrontation is needed." Rowan frowned. "I don't know if I'm explaining this correctly."

"So, because Amy was so angry, when she cast the spell she gave it a form. Basically, she made it into a thought form that was composed of millions of little pieces."

"Correct," Rowan said. "Like a hive of bees, with all their focus being on finding out who the 'other' woman or man is. The stinger comes out when they start fighting. And the virus makes the victim combative, absolutely convinced that their partner is cheating. They can't be reasoned with because they're sick—they're under the influence of the spell. The virus also infuses them with the anger Amy was feeling."

"And she's a hothead," I said. "So that anger will likely be overwhelming and irrational."

"Exactly. I'm not sure how she screwed it up, but screw up the spell, she did. From the list of components Granny gave me, I know exactly which spell she cast. It's not to bring back a lover, but to reveal the 'truth of their cheating heart'...that's the actual name for it." Rowan rolled her eyes. "People need to get a grip. Yes, betrayal sucks, but revenge is always better served with an icy heart than a hot head."

"Yes, Khan," I muttered, grimacing. Somehow, I had the feeling that Rowan could be as ruthless as they came when needed. "What do we do? Can you create a magical cure for it? Is there a potion that will help, or will the virus go away naturally?"

Granny sighed. "Unfortunately, it won't go away on its own. And every person who gets it will be contagious for at least two or three days. Since it spreads through touch, even a handshake is enough to put someone in jeopardy of contacting it."

"What happens if that person doesn't have a partner?"

"Then they won't necessarily be affected by it themselves, but they can still pass it on. We're going to have to disinfect the entire town at this point—there have been too many brawls, too many breakouts. And you know those people had to have touched a lot of people in their personal lives. There's no way to stop the spread at this point by going after individuals. Even a handshake can transfer the virus."

"What do we tell Dagda?" I asked.

"Anybody he picks up needs to be kept isolated from the public until we come up with a cure, so he may have to commandeer one of the local hotels and lock people in there." Granny shrugged. "There isn't much else he can do. If he lets them out the day after they get into a fight, they're still going to be contagious."

"That's not going to go over well. Not with anybody," I said. "So, how do we cure this? Can we cure it? You said it won't just run its course? And if we can't track it, do we have to treat the entire town?" If Rowan was correct, we were facing a host of problems. And I had the feeling she was seldom wrong.

"No, it won't run its course. There's also the possibility—like with all viruses, magical or not—that it will mutate into something else. And that—"

Granny's phone rang and she glanced at it. "Dagda. I'd better take this." She moved away as we continued to talk.

"Mutate? That could be either bad or good. So, curing it... can we achieve a cure?"

"We can create an antidote and, at this point, yes, the entire town has to be treated."

"Kool-Aid in the water system, right?" I couldn't help but flash back to some of the actions domestic terrorists and cult leaders used. "That doesn't sound right. We're taking away their choice."

"It may seem that way, but sometimes you have to take drastic measures to repair a situation." Rowan gave me a long look. The depth in her eyes bespoke years of experience far beyond my own. "You worked for the Crown Magika. You know that sometimes you're better off keeping certain information silent because of the effect it will have on the public."

I thought back to a few of the situations we had with rogue vampires. There were things I'd never breathed a word of, not even to Granny, because my oath to the Crown forbade it. There were run-ins I'd had that would have terrified everybody sitting in this room. Well, perhaps not Rowan, but what I'd learned about the underground organizations who were out to disrupt society—both human and Otherkin—was daunting.

"Right," I said, giving her a nod.

"We have a problem," Granny said, returning from the dining room. "The virus has now claimed a life. Owen Wilde-burns murdered his wife tonight because he claims she was cheating on him. Dagda has a crew over there now. He wondered if you'd be up to going over there, Marquette, and taking Dominique with you. If her spirit is still there, she may be able to tell us more than his men can find out about the murder."

I nodded. "As long as I can take this chair with me," I said, patting the arms of the wheelchair. "Call Colton," I told Granny. "He's always up for helping. Tell him we'll make him a homecooked meal to thank him."

I closed my eyes as Granny moved aside again. "Dominique!? Dominique? I need your help. Dominique?"

Within seconds, I felt the rush of cool air pass through me. When I opened my eyes, she was standing next to me. Dominique glanced over at Rowan and her eyes went wide. Rowan gave her a nod and I realized that she could see Dominique, too.

"Dominique. Would you go with me to a murder scene? We need to find out if the spirit of the victim is still around. It's fresh so she might be, though she might still be in shock, as well."

Of course, Dominique said. She glanced at Rowan again. *Hello, Mistress. I bid you a fair evening.*

"A fair evening, indeed. We'll see. But well met, Mistress Dominique. My name is Rowan."

Are you going with us?

"I am, if you don't object."

Not at all. You'll be a welcome ally. Dominique turned to me. *If you'll allow me a moment, I'll prepare.*

I wasn't sure just what she needed to do in order to prepare, but I waved her off and she vanished. "So you can speak with the dead, as well?"

"My primary magic is fire, but I'm one of those who can feel the energy of all elements and I'm also trained as a High Priestess." Rowan stood and stretched as the doorbell rang.

Granny returned, Colton following her.

"I barely made it a quarter of the way home before you called. You need my help?" He glanced around anxiously. "Is everyone okay?"

"Well, we are, but Dagda's dealing with a dead body. Murder victim." I decided that Colton needed to know what was going on—and then I remembered. He had been in a physical fight with the guy at the restaurant. "Rowan, Colton touched someone who has the virus. Is there any way to tell whether he contracted it?" And then another thought occurred to me. "And he touched me afterward. Am I going to get it?" I suddenly realized how easy it was for the virus to spread.

Rowan frowned. "Both of you should be wearing gloves. No skin-on-skin contact. You shook hands with just about everyone who showed up tonight, right? If you'll excuse me, I'm going to help clean up."

I nodded. "While we're gone, Granny, can you make a list of who was here? I wonder, if we're not in a relationship, if the virus can affect us."

"Virus?" Colton asked, his voice squeaky.

"Yes, I'll tell you in the car," I said.

Colton hoisted me up and Jillian pushed the wheelchair out to Colton's car. He placed me in the passenger seat as she folded up the chair and slid it into the back. Dominique settled herself in the backseat and we pulled out of the driveway.

Along the way, I let out a sigh. "If we get infected with this, I wonder how the hell it's going to present."

"You were going to tell me what this is all about," Colton said, shifting gears. "The way you were throwing around the word 'virus' in there kind of petrifies me."

"Okay, here goes. But you have to promise to keep quiet for now. This could lead to panic throughout the town." I told him what we had figured out. "So Rowan was saying that the virus might mutate. That's when we got the call from Dagda. We're now facing something that can push someone to murder, so..."

"So not good. But do you think it's the virus that caused Owen to kill his wife? Or could it just be that he had an explosive nature to begin with and didn't need that much of a push?"

"That's a good point." I pulled out my phone and texted the thought to Rowan. She didn't answer, which was fine. *Hands free or let it be*, as the Department of Transportation's slogan on cell phone use in cars went. "To be honest, I have no clue who Owen is. I've never met him, that I know of. So I have no idea what kind of person he is."

"Whatever the case, the fact that a spell can backfire into a virus is news to me. That opens up a whole line of questions. And I'm *witchblood* and I've never heard of this happening. Does the Crown Magika know about this possibility? How often does this happen? You worked for them. What have you heard?"

When he was hyper-focused, Colton could sound awfully demanding. But I understood his concern. I was thinking all the same thoughts.

"I don't know, to be honest. I worked in a different department. I was focused on catching rogue vampires and members of the Covenant of Chaos. I wasn't on the magical side of the operation, other than the magic needed to catch the offenders." Now Colton had me wondering just how much had been hidden from us over the years.

"Is there any way you can find out? Surely you must still be in contact with people there?"

I pressed my lips together, shaking my head. "That ship's sailed across the ocean. You have to understand that—even when we're in the middle of the operations there—we're on a need to know only basis. We're never allowed to talk outside of the agency about what we know. In fact, I had to sign a number of privacy oaths when I was discharged. And if I violate those, I could be brought up on charges. Worst-case scenario: execution. Best case: a stern warning and years of probation. So, even if I knew anything about spells turning into viruses, I couldn't tell you. But the fact is: I don't. And I'm not prone to lying."

We arrived at the scene, and Colton pulled alongside the curb. The house was set back on the lot. It was a two-story mansion, or—as we called them in the Pacific Northwest—a McMansion. Large two-story houses built on tiny parcels of land, crowded together. As I glanced up at the house, I saw a set of steps leading up to the sidewalk. I grimaced. I could feel the tension from here.

"Colton, I'll need you to help me up the steps." I glanced in the back seat. "Are you ready, Dominique?"

Ready to follow you. She slid out of the car, through the door.

Colton carried my chair to the sidewalk first, darting up the steps and unfolding it, then putting the brake on. He returned for me, lightly setting me in the seat. Once he locked the car doors, he pushed me to the house, where the front door was open and police officers were moving back and forth through it.

One of them stopped us, but when I told him who I was, he motioned for us to go on in.

"The chief is in the dining room. Go right in, but please try to avoid touching anything." The officer jerked his head toward the left.

Colton wheeled me and Dominique followed by my side, half in the wall, half out of it. I was finally getting used to seeing her half-inside objects. We approached the kitchen, and I heard Colton gasp. But I was used to gruesome scenes, so what was waiting for us didn't faze me. At least, no more than any blood-stained crime scene had.

At least vampires disappeared into a pile of dust when you staked them, but over the years, I had seen too many bodies left in the wake of the rogues.

The kitchen floor was covered with blood. Owen's wife was there, on the floor still, her arms stretched out so that she was in a T-position. There was a gaping wound in her chest—the blood had spread through her dress from the gash, blossoming like muddy petals over the white material. She had a startled look on her face, as though she hadn't been expecting her husband to stab her. The knife was on the floor beside her, and the officers were taking pictures and making notes.

Dagda turned as I entered, a bleak look on his face. "Thank you for coming. I know it's your birthday but—"

"Never mind that." I looked around at the rest of the room. "Did he confess?"

"Yes, in fact he called us after he killed her to turn himself in. He seems totally dazed, and all of the anger seems to have vanished. His anger against her, that is. I have him on suicide watch at the station because...well, let's put it this way. When we got here, he was sitting here crying. He's in shock. I don't know if he fully realizes what he's done." Dagda twisted his lip, shaking his head. "What the hell is going on?"

I wanted to tell him everything, but I decided to talk to Granny and Rowan before doing so. But first things first. "I brought Dominique. She'll have a look around to see if she can find...what was the woman's name again?"

"Vera. Vera Wildeburns. Owen and Vera have been married twenty years. They never had children, but they've been solid. I can't imagine..." He drifted off and a look of exhaustion crossed his face.

"Sit down and rest. This may take a while," I said.

Dagda reluctantly sat down while I turned to Dominique. "Please see what you can find. Her name is Vera."

I'll look. I sense someone upstairs, so I'll go find out who it is, Dominique said. She vanished through the ceiling.

I stared at Vera's body. She had been a pretty woman, in a simple way. Shoulder-length brown hair. Dark eyes. Angular features but with a gentleness that tugged at my heart strings. Chances were, Owen was firmly in the grip of the virus and that she hadn't cheated on him at all. All this crap, because Amy couldn't just deal with her marital problems like most other women. Some situations called for a hex or a binding, but others called for common sense. With Amy's anger behind the spell, no wonder it had spread out.

I motioned to Colton to sit and he did, gingerly turning so he didn't have to look at Vera's body. The forensics team finished up and the medical examiner motioned for them to bag her body. As they gently lifted her into the body bag, I bit my lip.

Life was so fragile—one strong puff could blow out the candle. Anybody, at any time, could find themselves on the other side of the Veil. One misstep, being in the wrong place at the wrong time, a blind corner on a busy road... So many people were just one step away from ending up in the morgue. And eventually, every one of us would take that last walk. Even though I tried to shake off the feelings, they clung to me like cellophane wrap, and I was finding it difficult to shake off the gloom.

Marquette? I found her. Meet Vera, if you would. Dominique appeared by my side, another spirit in tow.

Vera looked, in death, much as she had in life, at least as far as I could tell. Her eyes were glowing, and she was drenched in blood—some spirits took awhile before learning how to change their appearance. But she had a sad smile on her face and, as she watched the techs wheeling her away, her expression slid into melancholy.

I don't know what to do now, she said.

"Vera? I'm Marquette. I was wondering if you could talk to me about your death?"

She seemed to startle, then shrugged, a resigned look on her face. *I suppose. I have no clue what the hell happened.*

"Why don't you tell me about it?" I glanced at Dagda and Colton, both of whom had perked up. "She's here. I'm talking to her now. If you have any specific questions, feed them to me. I'm not sure if she can hear you—"

I can. I'm actually more aware than I expected to be after my death. Then again, I didn't expect for this to happen so soon. She hung her head, shrugging again. *I can't for the life of me figure out why he snapped.*

"So I gathered," Dagda said. "Ask her what happened, and if she has any clue why Owen did this. Also...if it helps, tell her he's in shock. I don't think he meant for any of this to happen, and I don't usually excuse the behavior of murderers."

Vera shuddered. *Murdered. My husband murdered me. That seems so...how can I pick up from there? Anyway, tell the chief that we were just eating dinner as usual. I made meatloaf and potatoes— Owen's favorite meal. You can see the remains on the counter. I happened to mention that I had seen Joel Bryant while I was out picking up the dry cleaning.*

"Joel Bryant? Isn't he a plumber?" I held up my hand when Dagda opened his mouth. He closed it again.

Yeah, in fact, he's a good friend of Owen's. I ran into Joel outside the dry cleaner's. But Owen exploded. He accused me of sleeping with Joel and then... Her face twisted and tears rolled down her cheeks. *Owen called me a whore and said he knew I'd been sleeping around. But that's a lie—I never cheated on him. Ever. I love him. I would never hurt him. Why did he think that?*

I waited for a moment, as she composed herself. "What happened then?"

He grabbed the knife that I was using to slice the meatloaf and began waving it around. I begged him to put it down before he hurt someone, but he swore at me. He said that he had a feeling someone had been trying to wreck his home, but he had no idea it was his own wife and his good buddy. He came after me. I tried to make it to the kitchen door—I kept thinking if I could just get outside, I'd be able to run to the neighbors. But he was fast. Owen's a little pudgy, but he's strong. Then, I heard an odd sound—like something hard hitting something soft...it was a horrible sound.

She pressed her arm against her stomach, looking sick. I wondered if ghosts could get ill—at least on an astral level.

After a moment, Vera continued. *The next moment, my chest started to burn and I felt a lot of pressure on it. I looked down. He had stabbed me. There was blood pouring everywhere. I held out my hands, begging him to stop, but he stabbed me again and again. Those attacks hurt more than when it first went in, but maybe because I realized what he was doing. Owen stabbed me over and over, until I began to feel numb. I remember feeling so weak. And then...I was on the floor and then...I was upstairs in the bedroom, staring at the bed. I stayed there, until Dominique found me.*

I turned back to Dagda and relayed the story, feeling like a grim messenger. "I need you to wait right here," I said. Turning back to Vera, I added, "You too. Talk to Dominique for a moment while I'm gone. Colton? Can you wheel me into the hall? I need to make a phone call."

I wanted to be able to tell Vera why Owen had killed her. She deserved at least that much. She deserved a lot more, but it wasn't in my power to give her a new grasp on life.

Once Colton took me into the hallway, I put in a call to Granny and explained the circumstances. "I know you said we shouldn't tell anybody until we decide what to do, but I really want to tell Vera and Dagda what happened. What if I make Dagda promise not to act on anything until we figure out what to do about this? I really don't want Vera going through the afterlife, blaming Owen. They loved each other. And you never know what she might take it into her head to do if she thinks he was out to get her."

"You just don't like it when the underdog goes unavenged," Granny said. "Let me talk to Rowan and I'll call you right back."

As I waited, I looked up at Colton. "This is so sad. I really believe they loved each other."

"They did. I know Owen and I knew Vera. They were devoted to one another." He sighed. "It makes me question the wisdom of ever getting married."

"Things happen...life progresses, though sometimes in such a chaotic matter that nothing seems fair." I paused as Granny rang. "Hey, what did you and Rowan decide?"

"Go ahead, but make certain nobody else can hear you. However, we think you should tell the medical examiner too, so they have the right information and can quarantine the bodies. We don't know if the virus remains active after death. Also, since Owen could be brought up on premeditated murder charges, Dagda needs to know this isn't his fault. It's the virus speaking. Tell Dagda and the ME we're working on a solution, but that we're not there yet."

As she hung up, I let out a long breath. At least Vera

would understand what happened. While it wouldn't make any difference in the outcome, it might give her the chance to let Owen off the hook, and prevent further damage to come.

I motioned to Colton. "Okay, go ahead and wheel me back into the kitchen." I dreaded the talk I was about to have. Gods only knew what Dagda would do—but I had to swear him to silence. This couldn't get out prematurely. Not when Terameth Lake was facing a full-scale crisis.

"*Crap.*" Dagda shook his head. "You mean this is all because of a spell that backfired?"

"A spell that backfired so explosively that it turned into a virus. Our best guess is that—the witch in question—was so angry at her partner that she didn't want anybody to be happy. And that emotion fused itself into the spell, or the magical virus." I glanced over at Dominique. I needed to ask Vera if she had met with Amy, or if Owen had. But I hadn't told Dagda that it was Amy who was responsible yet, and I didn't want to.

"Dominique, you know who I'm talking about. Ask Vera if they knew each other."

Dominique paused, then understanding flooded her face. *Oh, you mean Amy?*

I nodded. "Yes."

Did you know Amy Farnell? And if so, have you seen her recently? Dominique turned to Vera.

Vera nodded. *Actually, yes. She's a friend of mine and she came over last week for dinner. She was really upset—she found out that Cranston, her husband, has been cheating on her with a twenty-year-old bimbo. Some rabbit shifter without a brain in her body. I wanted to help Amy feel better. So...oh no. Are you telling me* she's *responsible for this virus?*

"I'm afraid so," I said. "Meanwhile, is there any way you can stick around for a while? I mean, if you're pulled to the Veil, that's fine. Of course we'd understand. But we may have a few more questions for you, if you don't mind?"

Vera laughed. *I'm not feeling in a hurry to race on out of here. I just... I wish we'd never met her. I wish that Owen hadn't... I just want my life back. But I guess that's impossible now. I never thought it would be over this soon.*

There wasn't anything I could say to make it better, so I left Dominique in the kitchen to console her as I asked Colton to wheel me back to the living room. We needed to do something before anybody else decided to escalate their anger to a murderous rampage. And that meant working fast and furious.

CHAPTER THIRTEEN

*R*owan stayed the night, sleeping up in the guest room. The next morning, Granny had made a hot breakfast, but I couldn't eat it—not before my appointment with the Aseer. I was tired, having been up till all hours of the night with Rowan and Granny, trying to figure out the best way to combat the virus. Dagda had tried to wheedle the info out of me about who started the whole mess, but I just told him to call Granny. After he talked to her, it seemed to shut him up for the time being.

Meanwhile, the three of us sat up until three a.m., tossing around ideas. By the time we went to bed, Rowan had promised she would text several of her friends about the matter.

I spent the night tossing and turning. When I did sleep, I dreamed about Vera's mournful gaze, and the sadness that had filled her voice.

Midnight and Sunshine curled up beside me, one on each side of my pillow, and I finally fell into a deep sleep. But I still woke up at eight, ragged around the edges, and I was even grumpier because I couldn't have my caffeine. But at least I could walk into the kitchen on my own steam. My knee was feeling sore, but not bedraggled.

As I dragged myself to the table where I tried to fill up on water, Rowan appeared, inhaling the scent of waffles and bacon. "I'm hungry, that smells wonderful," she said.

"You're cruel," I grumbled to Granny. "You know I can't eat anything this morning."

"I'll save some batter and make you some waffles and sausages when you get home. I'm not going to the shop today, at least not the whole day, so Rowan and I should be here when you get back." She looked at me. "Are you sure you're back in walking form?"

"Yeah, the knee's sore but it's on the mend. I promise I won't try any hot action moves, or run, or jog, or climb steps." I glanced at my watch. "I need to leave for the Aseer's. I'll see you after I'm done. Wish me luck!"

They both waved, their mouths full, as I headed out the door. I decided to keep the rental car another day or two until I was fully sure I could make it into and out of my truck.

The Aseer lived out toward Mt. Rainier—near the Prospector's Gulch ghost town. State Route 165 was problematic this time of year, at least that far toward the mountain, with potholes and washouts. A scary-ass three-hinged arch bridge crossed the Carbon River, but luckily the Aseer's house was shortly before the bridge. I didn't want to chance driving over the almost five hundred-foot-long one-lane bridge overlooking a two hundred fifty-foot drop down to the water. Not this time of the year. The snow and ice were already blanketing the mountain and her outlying areas, and ice on that bridge could be a deadly affair.

As it was, the narrow two-lane highway leading up to the ghost town was nerve-racking enough with the ravines and drop-offs to one side. As I hugged the inner part of the lane closest to the mountain, I was grateful I hadn't driven my truck. It could make it through the toughest of areas, but the car maneuvered along the road better and had less of a chance of rolling over should I hit a patch of ice and go sliding down the embankment. Hoping I wouldn't be called on to test my theory, I kept my eyes on the road and took it at a moderate pace.

The timber near the mountain was primarily tall fir trees —so tall that they bowed in the wind. The sides of the road were covered with fresh snow, though the road itself was wet and clear. I cautiously approached the shadowed areas, on the lookout for black ice.

As I took the curves, ascending the grade, I realized that I'd never really been up to visit Mt. Rainier for a leisure trip. I'd have to remedy that. The dormant volcano was wild and feral, beautiful and treacherous. There was an energy up here that I had never felt anywhere else.

Every time I drew near the mountain I felt like I was being watched, and I know I wasn't imagining it. I didn't know what kind of creatures were in the forest, but they were supernatural.

While there were all sorts of wild animals in the park, the feel of those watching was different. They felt ancient, studying me, as if waiting for me to make a single misstep. A deep hunger underscored the feeling, like an ache in a belly that more often than not went unfed. I was always cautious when I went into the wilds—I knew how easily people vanished in the national parks, and how many of those were never found. Not all of them disappeared due to natural causes.

As I sped toward the Aseer's, I wondered how the evaluation at my age would differ from the first time I met her. Did she have a secondary test to check for changes? I remembered her from our first meeting—she was a woman of indeterminate age. She could have been thirty or three hundred for all I knew. Then again, to a teenager, everybody looked old. But I remembered that the Aseer had long black hair and pale skin and she looked almost bloodless, with dark, mysterious eyes.

I slowed down as I neared the bridge, looking for the turnoff to her house. Then, a mile or two before the Fairfax Bridge, I saw the road leading up through the cliff face that ran along the inner side of the road. I turned onto the winding road, navigating the S-curves with caution as the snow began to fall. The road wound upward, toward the top of the mesa. The foothills to the Cascades would be called full-fledged mountains in other states, but here they were simply mild precursors to the main events—the massive range of stratovolcanoes that divided the state into the east— desert, and west—coastline.

Most of Washington's population lived on the west side, and the politics were as divided as the geography, with the west being primarily liberal, and the east side of the mountains far more conservative. The west coast brought in the majority of money for the state, but the east side raised the crops. And between the two, the Cascades held sway, with the ability to destroy the infrastructure should the massive plates that formed them decided to shift, or one of the volcanoes decided to blow.

At the top of the rockface, the road opened up into a town a quarter of the size of Lake Terameth. Prospector's Gulch was left over from the early days of mining, though now it was primarily made up of a few families who had decided to homestead during the early 1970s. What had begun as a few hippies scratching out a bare living on the land had turned into a small, self-sustaining community that produced most of its own electricity. There was a school—a charter school, but it was reputed to be a good one—and even an urgent care that sufficed for most uncomplicated injuries and illnesses. The local market sold mostly food raised by the community and was like a food co-op more than an actual grocery store.

The Aseer lived here, in an old brick house, if I remembered right.

As I navigated through the streets—the downtown area was about three blocks by two blocks and the houses spread out from there, quickly turning into a number of urban farms—I began to sense a looming shadow. We weren't even near the Carbon River entrance to Mt. Rainier, and yet I could feel the tendrils of energy reaching through the land, pulsing from the heart of the mountain.

The GPS in the car told me to turn right at South Main Street onto River Road, and so I did. A quarter of a mile later, I pulled into the Aseer's driveway. The house was brick, as I remembered it, but it no longer looked old. Or rather, it didn't look weathered. The brick had been washed and cleaned, and the one-story house looked comfortable and tidy. The yard surrounding it was covered with a couple inches of snow, but the fence and the trees and the eaves of the house sported a cheery display of lights that shimmered against the falling snow.

I gauged the slipperiness of the sidewalk and decided to cut across the lawn. I had a walking stick in my car and retrieved it, welcoming the extra balance it provided. As I cautiously picked my way across the yard, the door opened and the Aseer appeared. She looked exactly as I remembered her from nearly forty years ago, as though time had kept its hands off her. She smiled and pointed to the porch steps.

"I salted yesterday so they should be clear of ice," she said.

I nodded, grateful that they did, indeed, look free from ice. The snow was another matter, but she swept it away before I climbed the three steps leading to the porch.

"It's been a long time," she said, opening the door. "Come in, I'll make some tea—unless you prefer coffee?"

"Coffee would be good."

As I entered the house, the scents swept me back to when I was young. There had been a scent in her house—a fragrance that was both delicate but memorable—and I realized I'd forgotten all about it until now. But I'd never smelled anything quite like it since then.

"It's as though time stood still here," I said, looking around. The same furniture, the same feel, the same scent. "Are you immortal?" I was only half-joking.

She offered me a seat on the sofa. "If you need to use the restroom, it's down the hall, first door on the right. I'll fetch the coffee."

As she excused herself, I stretched and then settled myself on the sofa. I was nervous. I didn't like admitting that, even to myself, but it was the truth. But being nervous didn't bother me the way it did some people. Nervous had kept me alive many times. Nervous equaled caution, and caution had kept me out of a number of bad situations. Of course, there had been times where I'd stumbled into something bad without realizing it, but I had always tried to pay attention to my intuition.

The Aseer returned with a tray containing a coffee pot, a creamer and sugar bowl, two large mugs, and a plate of cookies. I cleared a spot for it on the coffee table—there was an array of magazines and books in the way.

"Please, help yourself," she said, moving to sit in the armchair beside the sofa.

I poured myself a cup of coffee and one for her, too. Adding cream and sugar to mine, I took a sip and nodded. "That's good. What brand do you use?"

"It's a brand called White Fang, grown by a family of wolf shifters. I've come to really like it over most big-name brands." She leaned back in her chair. "All right, so tell me why you're here. I remember you—I spent some time yesterday looking up your file. I'm surprised to see you back in Terameth Lake. I always pegged you for someone who would hit the road and not look back."

"I did." I took another sip of my coffee. "I went to work for the Crown Magika and spent the next thirty years chasing down rogue vamps and members of the Covenant of Chaos. But I was sidelined early this year when I ended up mangling my leg in an accident. Since I couldn't do my job anymore, and I didn't want to be a desk jockey, I came home. I'm staying with Granny Ledbetter."

The Aseer's face crinkled and she nodded. "I heard you were back with her. You were living there when you first came to see me."

"Right," I said. "That was before my mother bought a house for us. She died some years back," I added, staring at my cup. "I just turned fifty-three yesterday, and ever since I had the accident, I've been noticing my powers shifting. Granny urged me to come talk to you, so I decided to make an appointment."

"Fifty-three? That would be around the age when our powers do shift and reform. It's almost like puberty for our magic. Our powers have a growth spurt and often change. Have you noticed they're more powerful? Or just different?"

I was surprised. "I rather expected to be put through a battery of tests like when I was young," I said. "I did have a startling experience with Arianrhod."

"Tell me about it."

I told her what had happened and she made notes as I talked, but said nothing. I was beginning to feel a little tired by the time I finished. I yawned.

"I'm sorry, I guess I needed more sleep."

"Don't worry about it. As for tests, we're just going to

talk." She leaned forward. "You can relax. I'm not going to require you to perform for me. So, has anything else changed?"

"All right," I said, settling back. "Okay, here are two things that are new: I can talk to animals. At least, I can talk to my cats. And I don't mean like most people. They talk back. It's internal dialogue, though I can hear it in my head verbally, but they talk…like people. It's not a vague feeling or anything like that. It's just like we're talking now, only they're young so it sometimes feels like I'm talking to a little kid."

"Give me an example, if you can."

I pulled out a notebook. "I expected you might ask, so…" I read off to her a few of the conversations I'd had with Midnight and Sunshine.

She choked back a laugh. "They sound like quite a pair."

"Oh, they are, but is that normal? I mean, most familiars don't talk to their witches that way, do they? I always thought having a familiar meant you'd be in tune, not in an in-depth conversation on the pros and cons of beef over bison."

"Well, bison is leaner, but I agree with Midnight that beef has more flavor." She laughed, then. "I'm sorry, it's just… you're right, most witches don't have those sorts of conversations with their familiars. Most witches don't have *actual* conversations with their familiars. So that's a relatively rare power you've developed. It's not unknown, but it is rare. What else have you noticed?"

I shrugged. "I can talk to ghosts and see them, now. I mean I have full-fledged conversations with them. Our house ghost—Dominique—has helped me in investigating a few cases for the local chief of police. If I take her with me to a murder case, she can look for the spirit of the victim, and if they're around, get them to talk to me."

The smile slid away as the Aseer continued to take notes on what I was telling her. "Anything else?"

I frowned, trying to remember if there had been anything different. "I've always had luck on my side, for the most part, but my ability to sense energy is growing. All the way out here today I could sense the mountain and her power, and it spooked me, to be honest. It also feels like the powers that I can sense, can sense me as well. So I feel like I'm being watched, a lot."

I realized I was beginning to feel very relaxed. In fact, I was having trouble focusing. I set my coffee cup down, then stared at it. "What did you put in my drink?"

"Nothing that will harm you," she said. "Just close your eyes and put your trust into me."

I wanted to protest, but the fog began to take hold. Frantic, I searched my instincts, but nothing inside warned me against her. And since I didn't have much choice, I let out a long breath and leaned back, closing my eyes.

"All right," I murmured. "But if you hurt me, I'll make you wish you'd never me...me...met me." And with that, I found myself drifting up and out of my body.

I WAS DRIFTING OVER MY BODY, BUT I COULD SEE A STRONG silver cord attached from my spirit's heart chakra to my body's heart chakra. The pulse was strong and steady—and my fear faded away. She wasn't planning on killing me—if she had been, I'd be dead by now, given the extent of her power. No, she was just leading me on a journey, I thought, and for some reason she hadn't wanted me to prepare for it.

"Can you hear me?" Her voice echoed through the fog. "If you can, then nod your head."

Apparently I nodded, because the next moment she was whispering instructions.

"Now I want you to walk over the edge of the bridge. Can you see the bridge?"

I glanced around and—sure enough—I found myself standing near the Fairfax Bridge. I was on one end of it, and the dusk was falling all around me. The water roared by below, white water foaming as it churned its way through the gulch.

"Walk out to the center of the bridge and go to the right side."

I hesitated, then set one foot on the bridge. It trembled, though I couldn't see anything shake, and I realized what I was feeling was the water from below, careening into the trestles keeping the bridge aloft. The water had been carving a channel through the forest for thousands of years, and the hundred years that the bridge had stood was a faint blip on the face of history.

Moving out onto the bridge, I became aware of the energy surrounding me and the bridge. It was everywhere, the deep resonant beat of the mountain's heart. It flowed like blood through the trees, through the land, through the water. Massive deposits of andesite gave foundation to the foothills, ancient remains of the pyroclastic flows that the mountain had spewed out onto the land, overtaking the vegetation and settlements. One day she would roar to life again—it could be tomorrow or it could be outside of my lifetime, but she wasn't done yet.

As I neared the center of the bridge, then crossed to one side, I could feel the literal weight of the earth pressing down on my shoulders. I approached the guard railing and looked over, gazing at the roar of water below. It was calling me and I felt a strong pull to leap into its depths and let it carry me along. I had started to climb over the side of the railing when I heard the Aseer calling me. She was standing in the center of the bridge and walked over beside me.

"What do you see?"

"The water," I whispered. "It's calling me."

"But is it the water?"

I sat down on the railing and stared at the water, trying to pinpoint the call. There, it was—faint and yet insistent. But as I followed the summons, it dipped below the water, into the rocks that made up the riverbed. And as I dove into the core of the rocks, the voice sang from the invisible web, connecting everything—every rock, every tree, every shore, every drop of water. I glanced over at the Aseer.

"What's calling me? It's not the water like I thought, but it's not the earth either."

"The web itself—the power of magic. Can't you feel the power everywhere? You're hearing the spirit of magic, Marquette. It's calling for you to wake it up in yourself. You've ignored most of your powers except for honing your intuition most of your life. Now, it wants out. Why have you so long resisted your personal nature?"

I thought about it, realizing she was right. The magic was calling me, the energy surrounded me, and filtered through every strand of my being. I held out my hand and was immediately buffeted by the wind and snow, by the water and earth and the fire deep within the mountain.

"What am I feeling?" I whispered, in awe.

"You're feeling *life*, Marquette. This river is but one stream of energy in the whole design that makes up our lives. You can't wield power unless you understand its depths and heights. As you sink into the magic, you'll begin to learn where the changes in your nature lie."

At that moment, I realized she was right. I'd never paid much attention to magical energy. I adopted the look and the feel of my heritage, I carried a blade and a wand, but how often had I actively used my magic, other than my intuition?

"Intuition's a very real part of the power lurking inside

you. Remove the shadow of what you fear in order to tap into it successfully." She pointed to the river. "Go now, ride with the river and learn."

And before I could say a word, I was toppling over the edge, falling two hundred and fifty feet, toward the rushing river below. As I landed in the water, a shock raced through my system, and I opened my eyes.

CHAPTER FOURTEEN

*A*lmost immediately, the water tugged me down. I took a deep breath and let the undertow drag me below the freezing surface. The white water ran high, bouncing over the jagged rocks that had long ago been deposited by the glaciers as they slowly crept back north. The walls of the ravine were steep, slick with patches of snow. Even if I could swim against the current, I doubted I could climb the sides. But I wasn't here to find my way out. I was here to learn. If I bailed now, I wouldn't learn whatever lesson awaited me. I came up for air again, gasping. Even in astral form, the experience felt so real that I couldn't help but gasp for breath.

For a moment I lingered above the surface, treading water, until the icy fingers of the river rose up and dragged me back below the murky water. Gray with minerals fresh off the glacier for which it was named, the river was running so fast and so high above its normal level that there was no way I would have survived if I had fallen in while in my body.

I tried to focus less on trying to breathe and more on just letting the experience guide me. As I turned my focus away from myself, I began to see forms in the mineral-laden waters, like gray ghosts from long past—skeletal mermaids whose eyes shone with a pale blue light. They were frightening to look at, but they didn't attack me. Instead, I went on instinct and reached out to the nearest one, holding out my hand. She gazed at me with those glowing eyes and her bony fingers clasped mine.

She pulled me down and I followed her, offering no resistance. As we approached the bottom, a vortex appeared on the bottom of the riverbed. Swirling, it looked like a whirlpool of energy. I tensed but forced the worry aside. I knew I needed to dive deep, to swim down into the depths of the riverbed, to follow the currents of energy that roiled and boiled their way down the channel. The skeletal mermaid floated backward, waiting. I looked at her, and in her eyes I could see the challenge. She wanted me to go first. She wanted me to take a chance, to take the lead and leave fear behind.

I turned back to the vortex. The center was dark as the night sky with what looked like ice crystals and snowflakes swirling in it. I gathered my courage, telling myself that I would not die. This was all a vision quest, and while I could be hurt, chances were that I would just shake out of it if something happened. I didn't know if I was right, but I chose to believe that.

Aiming at the center of the vortex, I swam through, spinning as I hit the energy, like an arrow spinning through the air toward its target. I entered the dark center, the core of the whirlpool, and the currents took over. I lost control, flailing to keep my sense of balance, but that too was stripped away. The skeletal mermaid was behind me, and from where I swam, it looked like she—too—had lost control.

The water dashed me from side to side within the funnel. I half expected to be tossed out, lost somewhere between worlds, but every time I slammed against the side of the whirlpool, it felt like a thousand hands were pushing me back toward the center.

As long as I didn't panic, I'd be all right. I listened, straining to hear something over the roar of the water, but the churning was so loud that nothing could register through it. The channel seemed to go on forever, as did my wild ride. I bounced from side to side, then suddenly I was sliding on ice. I didn't even know if I was still underwater, but I slid along, whirling as the whirlpool swirled. The mermaid was beside me, her face placid and unreadable.

After what seemed like hours, I could see a glowing light from up ahead. I wanted to shout, to let the mermaid know we were coming to the end of the passage, but then I realized that I could no longer see her. The funnel through which I'd come was growing dark, and the only lights were the swirls of energy that were directly around me. As I slid along the channel, everything I had just passed through dropped off into a murky nothingness, cloaked in fog. And up ahead, a brilliant light emanated from the very core of the funnel.

As I steeled myself, I shot out of the channel, landing hard on a field of shimmering ice. The entire world seemed made up of frozen liquid. Everywhere I looked, I saw fields of snow, and vast walls of ice around the perimeter. I wasn't sure if I was inside, but then when I looked up, I saw the shimmering aurora dancing across the sky, blotting out the stars.

I turned, and there—once again—was Arianrhod, clad in her midnight cloak, cowled with her silver veil. She carried her silver staff, waiting near a particularly large ice formation.

"Where am I?" I asked, kneeling before her.

"You are in the core of your power."

"Ice? I have power over ice?"

"Speak less, and listen."

I pressed my lips shut and did as ordered.

She waited.

At first all I could hear was the creaking and groaning of the ice, but then as I waited, the groans turned to something else—it sounded like the song of the humpback whale, echoing from one ear to another. The deep, sonorous echo pierced through me, making me shiver in the way no amount of cold could. The ice sang to me, but more than that, the sounds lifted up toward the sky, and from somewhere far above, a crystalline sound echoed back—the delicate tones of windchimes and pale flutes. The stars were singing along with the ice, one chill void summoning another. The aurora added its own song, snapping and crackling in time to the cadence.

As above, so below.

The noise grew louder till it blotted out my surroundings, and I lost myself in the ancient call of the ice. It was everywhere around me, the frozen wasteland.

As I followed the thread of song, I began to recognize that there were concepts and thoughts behind the tune—not words, the ice and stars weren't talking in that way—but powerful questions were being asked, and the answers were being provided. I wasn't sure who was asking and who was answering—but the two extremes were exchanging equations and magical formulas. And the longer they spoke together, the more I began to understand.

I tried to turn off my thoughts, tried to step into the center of the exchange. Information flooded my subconscious, though I had no idea what I was learning or hearing. It was as though my body opened up, thirsty like a sponge, and I was absorbing knowledge in a way I'd never before thought possible.

I didn't know how long I stood there, or even whether I was cold or not. At one point I had almost ceased being aware of who or what I was, I was so swept up in the songs of the ice and the stars. But after a long while, I became aware of my surroundings again. Arianrhod was still standing there, silent, watching me.

"What am I supposed to—" I started to ask what I was supposed to learn, but as if rising up to answer me from within, I felt the icy chill of energy coil around my spine.

Not solely the power of the water, nor of the ice or stars, it was a mix of all three, and I felt it connect to the magic I used for intuition and guidance. Suddenly, I could see the strands of the Silver Web that were mine, and then—others as well. I could see the connections we made on the web. I cautiously reached out with my mind and touched one strand. Instantly, I saw Granny's face—I had found her web.

Suddenly terrified, I turned to Arianrhod. "I can't cut them out of the web, can I? Like you? I can't hurt them if I *think* about hurting them?" I didn't want power like that—I didn't want be responsible for anyone's life.

"No, it's not that simple and you don't have that scope of power. But this is how you work, especially now. You could have done this before, but you weren't able to tap into your full potential. Now that the energy has woken inside of you, you can learn how to use it."

She raised her hands and, as she did so, the ice around us began to sing again, a deep resonant sound that reverberated from outcropping to outcropping.

"Behold my realm. The stars, deep space, the ice, the aurora, the barren wastes covered by snow. This is your world, too, Marquette. You thought you lived in fire—in the heat of the chase. But the true power lies in the march of the ice, the long nights under the darkened sky when the Hunt rises. Fire may melt ice, but then the melted ice vanquishes the fire and flows onward, only to freeze again."

"Aren't both necessary to temper steel?"

"Yes, the balance is there and must be honored. But those of us who live under the night, who live in the cold and darkness, have a keen insight of the flow of time—one that fire, in its haste, cannot understand. We plan and we watch, we wait for the right time."

"So water works in the long vision of the world," I said.

"Nothing can withstand the Ocean Mother's flow. The world was born in her womb. Only later did the fires bring forth the mountains, and it was out of the water that land rose." She turned to me. "You must return to your body. Learn how to use the knowledge you received today. Meditate and ask for my help when you need it. I will aid you when the time is right."

And with that, she vanished, a sparkle of frost in her wake. I turned around, wondering how to get back to my body but the next moment, I found myself falling, surrounded by stars, and when I opened my eyes, I was in my body once again.

THE ASEER WAS SITTING BESIDE ME. I WAS SURPRISED TO find a blanket around my shoulders. I was shivering, even with the fleece throw tucked around me. The Aseer held out a cup—it was hot and smelled like apples.

Shaking, I took it and, with her help, sipped the fragrant cider. As the hot liquid raced down my throat, I accepted the fresh slice of bread with melted cheese that she tucked into my hands. Before I could bite into it, I winced as a hunger headache hit me deep in my third eye. With a soft groan, I bit into the slice of warm bread and cheese, wolfing it down.

The Aseer held out a plate, filled with several slices of creamy cheddar, another slice of bread, and a pre-sectioned orange. Without a word, I accepted it, eating as fast as I could politely do so.

"You're so hungry because you were out so far on the web.

When we go out too far, it hits our bodies and we burn through energy at an incredible rate." She paused, then asked, "Do you remember what happened?"

I tried to think, then it flooded back. The bridge, the water, the mermaid, then shooting into the ice caves or wherever I was. Arianrhod. The symphony between ice and stars.

"Yeah, I'm not sure what to make of it all, but I remember it. It's as though I went to a place that reminded me...well, of the way celestite feels when I hold it, or when I hold labradorite or nuummite." The stones were ones I had encountered a few times in the shop, and each time I had shied away because they scared me for some reason.

"They're tied to the energy of the web, of the stars and the aurora. They're linked to the outer reaches. Marquette, that's where your energy belongs." She gave me a soft, almost sad look.

I stared at her. For some reason, the thought terrified me. "I'm not sure what to think about that," I said. "I'm not sure what to...to *do* with it."

"You're good at persuasion, aren't you? At intuiting the right move ahead of time. You're good at sensing where someone will be?" She leaned back in her chair, pulling a throw over her legs, and I realized the temperature in the house was dropping.

I nodded. "Yes, why?"

"Because that's where you're heading. Your magic is deep within you. You won't need to be out in the woods, or near the water, or out in the winds or dancing around a fire. All you'll need is the willingness to travel out to the web and there, you will find your source and strength. Until now, you've done so on a limited basis, given what you've told me. You've assumed throughout the years that it's all been your intuition, but it's your innate magic that's been keeping you going. Now, you need to actually use it on a *conscious* level."

As I comprehended what she was saying, it began to make sense to me. "You mean that every time I made a move, every time I thought I was just lucky or that I just had good instincts, I've been drawing on magic?"

"On your magic in particular, yes."

I digested the information for a moment, then said, "If I could do that when I wasn't even trying, what could I do if I meant business?" And then another thought occurred to me. "Do you think my accident changed things? Is that why my magic seems to be getting stronger? And how does it play into being able to talk to the cats?"

"You're touching their webs directly. You are connecting with them on a purely magical level. As far as your other question, no—your accident didn't cause your magic to shift. Your magic shifting caused your accident. While you were out on your vision quest, I took a look at your life path. You were at a major crossroads during the time of your accident— a point where you'd soon have to choose between paths. You see, this kind of magic is rare, and it requires a lot more intro- spection. It works on an entirely different level. And you couldn't give it the time or focus needed if you continued on your path with the Crown Magika, not as an agent like you were." She held my gaze. "Your subconscious decided for you."

"Are you saying that the accident happened because..." I had a hard time accepting that I had caused it—that I had invited my own injuries. "I would never choose to be hurt—"

"You didn't choose being *hurt*. You chose the path of your magic. And since you wouldn't listen to your intuition, fate dealt its own hand."

I was trying to figure out what the difference was. "I'm not sure I understand."

"Say you were trying to decide whether to buy a blue dress

or a red one. You have to have a new dress, but these are your only options."

That seemed odd, but I decided to go with it. "Okay."

"On a subconscious level, you know you want the blue one, but you ignored your inner promptings. Maybe your subconscious knew that you were about to run across a killer who only kills women wearing red dresses. But you're still unsure. So, fate steps in and the red dress sells before you can buy it. You're left with the blue dress. Now you don't *have* a choice. Tell me, around the time of the accident—in the month or so before—did you have any feeling you should maybe slow down, maybe think about doing something else?"

I frowned, starting to automatically say "no" but then a memory crossed my thoughts.

I remembered sitting at my kitchen table one day, about three weeks before the accident, not wanting to take the new assignment. Something felt off about it, and I remembered being afraid. There was something about it that I didn't like. Inside, I kept thinking maybe I should take a vacation or a leave of absence for a brief time, but then my ego got the better of me.

Just as I was about to ask for a pass on the job, I discovered that I was one catch away from being top of the list. One more successful capture and I'd be the best in the agency. So I goaded myself out of taking a break, telling myself that I was being foolish. That I was being lazy. All thoughts of vacations and leaves of absence vanished.

"So, I *knew* I should back off, and I didn't listen to myself." I paused, then asked, "If I had asked them to give me a pass, would that have changed my life the way the accident did?"

"Not in the same way, and I can't ever tell you for certain, but yes—I believe it would have. So you see? You're on the path to controlling your magic, rather than letting it control you." She smiled. "And the strength of your powers are about to amp up, given your age."

Everyone who was of witchblood origin found their powers shifting around the age of forty to fifty. Like menopause for the spell-set, only instead of losing something, we usually gained strength or powers. I waited, but she remained silent.

Finally, I said, "So what should I do? Should I take classes or...do you understand what I'm saying?"

The Aseer laughed. "Yes, I do. Don't worry. I'll write up a plan for you—like a new exercise regimen for your magical muscles—and email it to you. If you have any questions, you can always ask me."

As I thanked her and left, a handful of cookies in hand, I realized that the experience was fading fast. It made me sad —it was like a dream that was vivid when you first woke up but it faded into the background the longer you were awake. Except on a core level, I knew that it had changed me, and now I just had to start directing that change instead of blaming fate for what life had dished out.

I shivered. It was snowing hard and I was grateful it was time to head home, before the storm kicked into high gear.

CHAPTER FIFTEEN

*B*y the time I was halfway home, the storm was blowing wild, with snowflakes going everywhere. I was deep in thought as I entered the town limits and cautiously navigated the streets. My time with the Aseer had answered a number of questions, but it had left me wondering. I kept coming back to the thought that—if I'd listened to my intuition—I could have spared myself a permanent disability.

But then, I don't know that. This might have happened in some other way. Perhaps this was woven into my web no matter what.

I sighed. I didn't want to believe that, but again—the nagging feeling that I was onto the truth struck me. Maybe no matter what I had chosen, no matter what I had done, I would have ended up hurt.

That's the thing, isn't it? We never know what's important and what isn't unless something happens to give us proof later on. It's all one big crapshoot.

And then, Arianrhod's voice echoed through my head again, though I wasn't sure it was actually her. It might have been my intuition using her as a mouthpiece.

Even the smallest pluck of a thread out on the web can send shock-waves through the universe. A butterfly's breath can make men tremble. Everything is connected, never forget that. No matter what you think is important, never overlook the simple things, the simple actions.

As a child inhales its first breath, so the grandmother exhales her last breath. As a star dies, another star is born. The cycles move. The world turns. The seasons grow lush and abundant, then wither and die, fallow stalks on the wind until spring once again arrives. Every movement we make initiates into being a chain of action.

As she fell silent, I realized I was back home. I turned into the driveway, parked, and then cautiously made my way to the back porch, my mind so filled with a whirl of thoughts that I barely knew where to begin.

I WAS SURPRISED TO FIND GRANNY STILL AT HOME. "WHAT about the shop?"

"I hired a friend to watch over it today. I thought I should be here when you returned," she said.

Grateful she was, I slid into the rocker, setting my crutches to the side. Even though my knee was feeling stronger, better to be safe than sorry. The last thing I needed was to fall on the slippery sidewalk.

"So, I learned quite a bit about myself." I looked up to meet her gaze.

"What's changed? What kind of magic is coming to the forefront?"

"Well," I said, "I didn't expect this. Let me tell you what happened." I proceeded to tell her everything I could remember. Even though the experience had faded and was now dreamlike, I was able to see it in a clearer light. Perhaps because I had had the time to emotionally distance myself so that I could recall the important facets.

Granny listened carefully, nodding off and on. "So, you're one of the rare ones. You're born to celestial magic. Bound to the web like Arianrhod. That's a special gift, you know."

I nodded. "The Aseer told me. I—" I was about to go on when the doorbell rang. "Are you expecting anyone?"

Granny sighed. "Yes. I invited Amy over."

"Oh cripes, Amy Farnell?"

"Yes, the same. I figured if anybody could get away with talking to her about the love spell, I could. Well, and Rowan. Rowan's still here—she agreed to stay on to help out for a few days. Will you answer the door while I get her? I don't want you climbing the stairs."

As she headed toward the stairs, I reluctantly answered the door.

Amy Farnell was a pretty girl—prettier than I'd expected. By the description of her demeanor, I'd expected to see someone with overly pinched and angular features, someone who looked like an angry bird. But Amy was radiant. She had hair the color of spun gold, and a flawless complexion. She was on the thin side, but well-proportioned, and stood around five-seven. Her eyes were green like a sunlit forest, and as she stepped into the house, I could feel a wave of energy surrounding her. I wondered if I would have been able to feel it this morning, before I had visited the Aseer.

I held out my hand, introducing myself, but as she clasped my fingers, I shivered. As pretty as she was, her hand felt like charred meat—still steaming. Her fingers were hot and dry, and I was surprised they weren't burned when I looked at them.

In a quick vision, I saw someone for whom all liquid in their body had boiled away. Amy felt like a husk. A beautiful husk, but still a shell. And within the shell, I sensed a seething resentment, an anger that never went away.

"Come in," I said, keeping my gaze locked on her.

"Granny invited me over," she said.

"She mentioned it to me," I said.

I led her into the living room, motioning for her to sit down. "So, I don't think we've had the pleasure of meeting," I said. "I'm Marquette Sanders. I'm Granny's goddess-daughter and I work at the shop with her part-time, but I guess I haven't been down there when you've been there."

"I suppose not," she said, her manner a little more formal than was comfortable. She felt stiff, aloof. Nothing about her energy matched the golden girl on the outside.

I struggled to think of something to say. I didn't want to give Granny and Rowan away before they returned with what we suspected, but I had no clue what to talk about and Amy was as helpful as a slug. Finally I decided to tackle the age-old topic of the weather.

"Do you think we'll get more snow?" I glanced out the window where it was still blowing up a gale.

"I have no clue," she said. "I'm sure that if we do, we will, and if we don't, we won't." Now her tone was haughty, setting me on edge. I bristled, but tried to keep myself civil.

"What do you do?" I asked, deciding to run down the gamut of typical questions. If she told me to mind my own business, I'd shut up and leave her stranded in the living room while I went into the kitchen and made myself a sandwich.

"I'm married to Cranston Jones."

She was succinct, I'd give her that. Apparently, in her world, marriage was a career in itself. She also seemed thoroughly uninterested in talking to me.

"I see. That sounds like...interesting *work*," I said, unable to help myself. I knew it sounded catty, and in fact—it *was* catty, but I was very quickly coming to dislike Ms. Amy Farnell. Or, rather, *Mrs. Cranston Jones*. I wouldn't be surprised if she'd be the type to get insulted on being addressed as a woman in her own right, without the need to attach herself to being her husband's property. I *was* surprised, however, that given what prestige she bestowed on being Cranston's wife, she hadn't taken his name.

She rolled her eyes, then looked at the wall, signaling that our conversation was at an end. Both relieved and yet insulted, I headed toward the kitchen. But as I was about to leave the living room, I heard voices on the staircase. Granny and Rowan appeared.

Granny tossed a glance over my shoulder at Amy, then looked at me.

I rolled my eyes, giving her a little shake of the head.

"Come back in with us," Granny said, sliding her arm through mine.

"I'm hungry," I countered, uninterested in being part of a tête-à-tête. I had already taken a strong dislike to Amy and wanted as little to do with her as possible.

"Food can wait, dear," Granny said, holding on tighter.

"You owe me for this," I whispered.

Granny just grinned and I realized I wasn't going to get out of the meeting.

"Dinner on me, wherever you like," she whispered back.

"*Two dinners*, wherever I like," I countered.

"Deal. Now come on."

I grudgingly let her steer me back into the living room. Amy glanced up, her gaze landing on Granny. Immediately, she looked more animated, as though the amateur act was off the stage and the main event had begun. Once again, I felt a growl rise up inside but I squashed it down.

As we settled ourselves in our seats, Rowan entered the

room. She took one look at Amy and I felt the energy shift. Rowan glanced over at me and gave me the faintest of eye rolls and I felt vindicated.

"Granny, what can I do for you? You wanted to see me?" Amy focused solely on Granny, not even asking who Rowan was.

I started to clear my throat, but Granny took hold of the situation. "Amy, this is my goddess-daughter, Marquette—"

"We've met," Amy broke in.

"Yes, well then. This is Rowan Firesong. She lives in Moonshadow Bay."

As Granny introduced Rowan, Amy flinched. She slowly turned around to look at Rowan and licked her lips.

"How do you do?" Amy asked. She added, "I've heard of you. You're supposed to be the strongest witch in Moonshadow Bay."

"I am. In fact, I'm the strongest witch in the area. Granny asked me here because there is an issue we need to talk to you about." Rowan seemed as impressed with Amy as I was.

Amy's look turned from blasé to concerned. "What happened? Did I do something?"

"The fact that you ask that indicates you know what we're about to say." Rowan wasn't taking prisoners, that was for sure.

Amy looked like she was about to hyperventilate.

"Do you know what's been happening around town?" I decided to ask. "Have you heard what's going on down at the jail right now?"

Amy stared at me as if I had just appeared out of nowhere. "I'm not sure."

"Did you cast a spell against your husband?" Granny asked. "Or a spell in general, to bring any extracurricular activities he may be involved in to light?"

The answer was clear as day, but Amy wasn't forthcoming. "I'm not sure what you're talking about. Why would I cast a spell against my husband?"

"*Don't play with me, girl.* I have a record of the spell ingredients you bought from me about ten days ago. I can tell you right now, that spell wasn't intended to win friends and influence people. You are either trying to uncover evidence that Cranston has been cheating on you, or you set a spell to prevent him from doing so. You need to tell us *exactly* what you did."

At that, Amy puffed up. "Why should I tell you anything?"

"Because whatever it was you did backfired. And now someone is *dead*." Rowan stood, crossing her arms as she glared down at the woman.

Amy shook her head, her golden hair glittering under the lights. "How did you know it's because of something I did? Couldn't someone else have cast a spell that got out of hand?"

Rowan pointed to Amy's hands. "Hold out your hands and let me see them."

Hesitating, Amy started to sit on them instead. But when Rowan cleared her throat and leaned in, she slowly held them out, palms up like a guilty schoolchild. Rowan ran her own hands over the top of Amy's palms, not touching them. A faint light swept through the air between them. Immediately, I could see hundreds of tiny squiggles squirreling around on Amy's hands. They were dots of light, a lot like fireflies, but they seemed embedded in her skin.

I gasped, pointing. "What on earth is *that?*"

"The virus." Rowan glanced over at Granny. "She's Ground Zero, all right." She turned back to Amy. "It's no use. The jig is up. Tell us what's going on. We need to know what you did so we can fix it."

A sly look slid into Amy's eyes. "I still don't know what

you're talking about, not exactly. But yes, I cast a spell on my husband. I know he's been cheating on me, and I cast a spell to prove it. Only it didn't work. And it turns out, I didn't need it in the end. I walked into the bedroom the other day, unexpectedly. I was out on a shopping trip and when I got home, I found him in our bed with some bimbo, eating her out."

"Did you do anything else?" Rowan asked.

Her eyes narrowed. "Fine. You want to know? I grabbed the spell candle I was planning on using to find out if he'd been cheating on me and I lit it in Circle. I was going to cast a vengeance spell on him, but instead, I broke down and started venting to the gods about how love fucks everything up and nobody can trust anybody."

Amy flounced back against the cushions, staring at her hands. "He deserved it. You can't trust any men. They're all a bunch of cheaters, and they're all out to break your heart. I wished for them all to catch some STD and die."

Rowan and Granny glanced at each other, then Rowan let out a huge sigh. "And you said all of this in Circle with a spell candle burning?"

Amy nodded. "Yes. I keep the Circle up so that if I need to do any spur-of-the-moment magic, it's always ready."

I could see the sparks flying around Amy. I closed my eyes and did my best to glance at her threads on the web. They were flaring, as though they were solar flares or eruptions. They were so bright and neon white that it was hard to look at them. I winced, turning my head.

"What is it?" Rowan asked me.

"She's flaring like crazy out on the web. No wonder the energy escaped."

"What do you mean?" Amy asked, leaning forward. "What's all of this about?"

"You poured so much energy into your anger that you

created a magical virus. You basically gave it life and it's been spreading. You know perfectly well what's been going on with Dagda and the jail, that people are being arrested right and left for fighting with their partners. Your outburst is *directly* to blame." Rowan didn't relent, that much I'd say for her. In fact, I decided right then and there that I never wanted her angry at me.

"Rowan's right," Granny said. "Now we have to figure out some sort of magical antidote. Or some sort of magical vaccination."

"So a few witchblood are going ballistic over the relationships. Isn't that easy enough to deal with?" Amy seemed to have no remorse for what she done, or perhaps she didn't even have a clue of how important this was.

"You're missing the point, girl!" Rowan sighed. "This can infect non-magical people as well, and it has, from what I gather. You're putting a lot of people at risk, and we have to put a stop to it now." She glanced at Granny. "We'll need to talk to Dagda about a quarantine. People can't be running out of town or they're going to spread it farther."

I pulled out my phone. "I'll call him and ask him to come over."

"Let's wait until we have a clearer picture of what we're facing," Rowan said. "Then we can tell him."

Amy had quieted down. For the first time since she walked through the door I saw a trace of remorse in her eyes. "But how could I have done this? Wouldn't it take a trained witch in order to effect something of that magnitude? I don't have that much power."

"Not really. And you *do* have a tremendous amount of power in you. I'm surprised you were never trained. What did the Aseer tell your parents?"

Amy bit her lip, all arrogance sliding away. She nervously

twisted her hands. After a moment, she spoke. "Do you mean that? Do you really mean that I have a lot of power?"

"Of course I do. You wouldn't have been able to spread this like a virus otherwise," Granny said. "Why?"

But I knew—out of the blue, I knew what was going on. "Your parents never told you that you have power, did they? They never told you what the Aseer said, and I'll bet you never heard anything directly from the Aseer herself."

And then, right before our eyes, Amy deflated like a punctured balloon.

"I'm only half witchblood. The man I told everyone is my father is really my stepfather. My father—my blood father—disappeared when I was young. My mother told me he was human. My stepfather warned me never to talk about my heritage. He always insisted he was my real father to other people."

"Why on earth..." Rowan frowned. "What reason did he give?"

"He said he would be disgraced if his friends found out that my mother had an affair and got pregnant with me. I'm the family secret, you see. And my father—my stepfather—was so hard on me every moment of every day. I could never do anything right. I kept trying to make sure I was on top of all my studies. And of course, they couldn't send me to an academy since I was only half witchblood. I would have been found out. Hell, when I brought home anything other than an 'A' he punished me. Meanwhile, my mother was trying so hard to apologize to him that she never stood up for me."

I glanced over at Granny, my anger melting away. Amy was a disturbed young woman, and she needed guidance.

"We'll need your help, you know," Rowan said, modulating her voice into a soft tone. "Are you willing to help us?"

Amy nodded, tears slipping down her cheeks. "However I can, yes. I'm sorry, I never meant for this to happen."

And on that note, Granny motioned for us to follow her into the kitchen. At least we knew what was going on. Now we had to figure out how to deal with it.

CHAPTER SIXTEEN

I put in a call to the Aseer, asking her if she still had Amy's records. When children went to her, their parents were called in first, and then the child. But since Amy was supposedly only half witchblood, and her folks hadn't wanted her to know, she hadn't been told.

"There should be a law against keeping a child's heritage and abilities from them—how else can they learn how to handle their power?" I muttered, waiting for the Aseer to pick up.

"It's the perk of being a parent—even when it's to the detriment of their children," Granny said.

The Aseer came on the line at that moment, and I explained that Amy was here and we needed to know what her powers were. "I'd like to put Amy on the line so you can tell her what you found when you examined her," I started to say, but Amy tapped me on the arm.

"Put her on speaker phone. If you need to hear, too, then that would be easiest. And I'm in shock so I might forget something important." Her bravado was gone, replaced by a concerned desire to help. It once again struck me how much insecurity could stunt emotional growth.

"You don't mind?" I asked.

"No, I'd rather you do it that way."

I punched the speaker function and set my phone where everyone could hear it. "All right, we're here—Granny, Amy, Rowan Firesong—I don't know if you know her but—"

"Rowan! What are you doing there?" The Aseer's voice echoed into the room.

"Trying to put out a wildfire running through town. Granny, why don't you explain to the Aseer what we're facing and why we need to know what Amy's powers are. That might help her remember things that might otherwise seem insignificant." Rowan gave Granny a nod.

"Good idea," Granny said. She explained what was going on. "So, we need to know what powers Amy has that could have turned a spell into a virus."

"Oh my," the Aseer said. "Well, let me get her file. I always keep notes from the examinations just in case something like this comes up later." She put her phone on mute.

As we waited for her to return, Amy chewed on her lip. "I can't believe I have enough strength to do something like this. I'm afraid to think, now. I never would have been so rash if I knew something like this was even possible."

"It sounds as though you had a rough childhood," I said.

She felt raw around the edges, her nerves frayed and more than a little shell-shocked. And now that her façade had come down, I could sense the underbelly of her psyche—not evil, but cloaked in shadows, filled with memories long pushed down into the dark.

Amy glanced at me. "Yeah, I did. As I said, my stepfather punished me for existing. Why my mother stayed with him, I have no idea, but she did. I used to beg her to leave him, you know. He pushed her around, treated her like dirt. And he treated me like...well...when I did something well, it set a standard and anything less was never good enough. I held myself back in school so I wouldn't have to struggle to keep up with myself."

"You underperformed on purpose," Rowan said.

Amy nodded. "I was a solid B- student. I could have gotten As but I knew that the moment I started raising my GPA, if anything happened to make it fall or if I brought home a C, I'd be punished for slacking. I learned how to mute myself."

At that moment, the Aseer returned. "I'm back," she said, the sound of papers rustling in the background. "I have your chart, Amy. I remember you, specifically, because you were so confusing to me. Your parents insisted you were only half witchblood and they were only having you tested to confirm that fact."

"But I *am* only half witchblood," Amy said.

"No, you aren't. You're full witchblood." She paused, then added, "I know you think your blood father was human, but he wasn't."

"Well, my stepfather couldn't have been my birth father—he was sterile. My mother told me," Amy said.

"Yes, we—the Aseers—also track lineage. Neither your stepfather nor the man you thought was your father could be your birth parent. But I talked to your mother in private. She's dead now, isn't she?"

"Yes," Amy said. "But my stepfather's still alive."

"Well, I'm going to tell you since you're an adult now. Your blood father was actually an incubus. You are part demon, my dear. I know that's a lot to take in—"

Amy burst out with a "What?" that drowned out the Aseer.

Rowan and Granny both sat speechless, staring at her. I groaned and rubbed my head. No wonder Amy had more power than she thought.

After a moment, Rowan said, "That would give her the ability to create a virus, all right."

"What the hell do you mean? I'm part *incubus*?" Amy looked as confused as I felt.

"No, you're half succubus. When an incubus sleeps with a human or a succubus, the child is either full or half succubus if it's a girl. Incubus if it's a boy."

"Oh...so if I had been a boy, I'd be part incubus?"

"Yes. Being half demon gives you more than enough power to torque a spell to the wrong side if you're angry enough. I remember telling your parents about your heritage. They were so angry—or rather, your stepfather was. I'm not quite sure what went down, but your mother looked like she wanted to disappear beneath the floor."

"She must have been terrified. My stepfather had a horrible temper and he's a strong witch himself." Amy frowned.

"I tried to break it to them easily, and I wanted to talk to you. Your kind of power needs training. But neither one of them would hear of it. They insisted they'd handle matters and I didn't have any jurisdiction to counter them. Neither did I have the leeway to approach the Court Magika. I thought about talking to you, Granny, but that could have resulted in me getting my own powers stripped away. Confidentiality issues, you know."

We spent the next fifteen minutes piecing together what we could. Apparently, Amy's mother had been keeping not just one, but several affairs secret, including one with an incubus. And *that* tryst resulted in pregnancy.

"So, you're the Aseer, do you have any clue in how we can reverse a spell that backfired and turned into a magical virus?" I asked. If anybody knew how to counter magic like that, the Aseer should.

She paused. "So that's what this is about?"

"Unfortunately, yes." Rowan told her about the virus and how we thought it was working. "It's spread far enough now that we can't just muzzle the spell."

"And you have no idea how many people have been affected?" the Aseer asked.

"No. Is there something we can put in the drinking water? Is there any way we can take care of this without notifying the public?" Granny's expression was strained.

"There is a way to create an antidote, but you're going to have to administer it individually. If you can notify the townfolk to come get their doses, so much the better. Amy, tell me exactly what you did and what spell components you used. Then I should be able to figure out the counterspell."

Granny motioned to me. "Go talk to Dagda. *In person*, not over the phone. He needs to figure out a plan that will encourage people to take the antidote. We'll have to notify Moonshadow Bay and Whisper Hollow to keep an eye out in case anybody left town and spread this wide."

"Well, we can stop anybody from leaving for now. I'll have him shut down the exits. I'll talk to you later." I grabbed my crutches and gingerly headed for the door.

Dagda would have to deploy officers to close down the exits, as well inform the public somehow without causing a panic. I couldn't wait to see how difficult that was going to be.

Dagda looked up as I hobbled through. "What are you doing on your feet?"

"I'm better—but I'm using my crutches just in case. Listen, I need to talk to you privately. It's important. We know what's going on. But this is one fine mess we're all in."

He offered me a seat, then hurried to close the door to his office. "Coffee?"

"I'd love some."

"All right, what's up?" Dagda met my gaze as he poured a cup for me and waited.

"We know what's happening with all the lovelorn spats lately. And it's not a simple fix."

Dagda leaned back in his chair. "So, you found out the fix?"

"Yes, and...no. Someone cast a spell and it backfired. Now, we're dealing with a magical virus that can affect anyone in the community. We need you to immediately dispatch officers to block off the exits out of town. We can't risk letting this spread outside the borders of Terameth Lake."

As his jaw dropped, I began outlining what the Aseer, Rowan, and Granny had figured out. I had barely finished when he was reaching for the intercom.

"Hailey? Get in here now. If you see Geoff, tell him to stick around." He looked at me. "This is the stuff of nightmares. It might not be a fatal virus—"

"But it is. Vera's murder? That's a direct result of this virus." I paused, then said, "She—the person—feels horrible about this. I imagine people are going to be coming after her with lawsuits and maybe even threats. We may need to sneak her out of town."

"Are you sure this wasn't deliberate?" At my look, he backtracked, holding up his hands. "Okay, I just needed to ask. I wouldn't be much of a police chief if I didn't, would I?"

"I suppose," I said. "I thought maybe it was deliberate when I first met her, but she's had one hell of a rough life, and given she had no clue she was part demon until today, well, that's enough to frost anybody's soul."

"Really came as a surprise, hmm?"

The memory of Amy's face haunted me.

"I've never seen anyone look so devastated in my life. After she already dealt with her stepfather's disapproval and demands all through her childhood, and her mother didn't protect her, well, this was like another major blow. If she had been told from the time she was assessed, the Aseer could have given her exercises to control her powers. But to find out in this way has to be a major shock."

"I feel for the woman, but the aftermath is a mess and we're the ones left dealing with it. I'd like to have words with her parents, I'll tell you that."

Sometimes I could so easily see Dagda as a father—he had a strong protective nature that came from his bear shifter heritage, no doubt. Bear shifters were among the most protective parents around, although if they felt one of their children stepped outside the lines, they could turn into monsters.

I was about to agree with him when the door opened and an officer peeked in.

"You rang, boss?" She was tall and thin, with a weathered look on her face. I wouldn't want to try to take her down.

"Hailey, I want you to gather as many officers as you can and set up roadblocks at all exits. No one is allowed to leave the city limits." Dagda frowned. "What the hell should we tell them?"

That was a good question. "Tell them we're...hell, I don't know." I wasn't the one in charge.

"Tell them that we're searching for a dangerous subject and they're safest in their homes. That we can't allow anybody to leave town. If they give you grief, bring them in." Dagda sighed. "I just want this over and things back to normal."

"I'll head back to see if I can help Granny and Rowan. The minute we have the antidote ready, we'll bring it down. Can you round up everybody who was affected by the virus?"

Even if they had calmed down, chances were good they were still carrying the bug and could potentially spread it.

"I'll have my men gather them up. What are you going to do about those who don't want the antidote?" Dagda frowned. "I suppose everyone in town should receive it. What about kids?"

"We'll know more as soon as Rowan and Granny get it underway. Maybe phrase the request so they think they've been poisoned. I think they'd respond better than if you call it a virus—folks can be weird that way." I stood. "All right. I'm heading home. You do what you can from here."

As he escorted me to the door, I heard police cars from outside screaming away, sirens blaring. "Sounds like Hailey's got the ball rolling," Dagda said.

"Good. We need every advantage we can get."

As I carefully made my way back to my car and slid into the driver's seat, I could only hope that Granny and Rowan had managed to find a fix for the spell, and that we'd manage to contain it within the borders of the town.

CHAPTER SEVENTEEN

I arrived home to find Granny and Rowan elbow deep in components on the kitchen table. Amy was sitting there, still looking traumatized. They glanced up as I entered the room.

"Well, Dagda is putting up roadblocks. We've decided that if we call this an antidote to a poison rather than a vaccine, it will trigger more people to haul their asses in for treatment." I sat down in the chair that Amy pushed out for me.

"How are you doing?" I asked, turning to her.

She shrugged. "Better, I guess. I'm not in quite so much shock. But I have no idea what to do come tomorrow."

I hesitated, not wanting to mention what Dagda and I had talked about, but I felt like it was necessary. "Dagda and I discussed something that you should think about. When word gets out about this—and no matter how much we try to keep it silent, you know someone will find out—you might be facing a lot of community...anger."

She closed her eyes and let out a slow sigh. "I wondered about that. Even though I didn't mean to, I caused a lot of

havoc and damaged...well...I have no idea how many relationships."

I didn't want bring it up, but she had to know. "And there
was one death related to the virus—Vera Wildeburns. Her
husband Owen snapped and killed her."

Amy let out a little moan. "That's right. Somebody died
because of me." Her eyes welled with tears and she buried her
face in her hands. "I destroyed someone's life. She was my
friend."

I wanted to comfort her, to tell her it wasn't her fault, but
in truth, it was. She hadn't meant for it to happen, but indi-
rectly she had set into motion the events leading to it.

"Here now," Rowan said, setting down the large, tubular
roots she was peeling with a paring knife. "Look at me." She
settled herself in front of Amy and reached out, holding the
woman by the shoulders. "Come on, look at me."

Amy looked up, her face streaked with tears. "What?
What can I do to make this better? Death is one thing you
can't make right."

"No, but I'll bet you if you made it a mission to give talks
to students about how misusing magic—about how using it
carelessly—can backfire, it might prevent someone else from
making a fatal mistake."

"Aren't you being a bit rough? After all, Amy was just
trying to find out if her husband was cheating on her." I felt
like I needed to step in. As much as I had disliked her in the
beginning, now I felt empathy for the girl. Though she was a
grown woman, she still seemed like a fragile young girl who
was so afraid of being punished for never being good enough.

"But you already knew, didn't you?" Rowan gazed into
Amy's eyes. "You knew he was a cheat and a poor excuse for a
husband."

Amy worried her lip, but nodded. "Yes, I knew. But...he

picked *me*. Out of all the women he could have married, he chose *me*."

"And it made you feel wanted and loved," Rowan said with a sigh. "It made you feel—"

"*Worthy*. But you're right, I knew. I knew that he was cheating on me even when we were engaged. I knew it would take a miracle to make him stop but it didn't prevent me from hoping. He was the biggest catch in town, and finally someone important had noticed me—not only noticed me but chose me out of all the women he could have had." Amy leaned over, sobbing uncontrollably. "I just wanted him to love me."

As Rowan attended to her, I headed into the hall, toward the bathroom. Dominique was there. *I need to talk to you, Marquette. I'll wait.*

She politely waited outside the door while I used the toilet. After washing my hands, and splashing some cold water on my face, I headed back out.

I may be able to help that young woman. I've been talking a bit more to Vera.

I blinked. "You went back there to talk to her?"

Yes, I like her. We're going to keep in touch. She wants Amy to know that she doesn't blame her for her part in this. Vera told me that Owen wasn't quite the upstanding man she thought. She's asked me to have you tell the chief to dig up the rose bushes in the back garden.

I wasn't sure I liked the way this was going. "What is Dagda going to find?"

Two more bodies. Owen had a taste for young women. Vera introduced them to me when I went over there this afternoon. They were hitchhikers and Owen picked them up on the highway. They never made it out of his house.

I stared at Dominique, not entirely sure what to say. "Well...this is a new development. Are you telling me that

Owen killed two young women. Wait, how young are we talking?"

One, her name is Lindsey, is seventeen. Marabeth is...was...eighteen. They were headed down from the park, hitchhiking, when Owen picked them up. He promised to drive them into Puyallup, but first, he asked them if they were hungry. They stopped at his house. Vera was at work. He drugged them, raped them, and then strangled them before burying them in the back yard. All before Vera got home. So even though Owen killed Vera, thanks to her, it will expose two more murders. Vera doesn't know if he committed any others. Dominique sounded so proud of herself I almost laughed, but that would have been entirely inappropriate, plus the whole subject made me queasy.

I pulled out my phone and called Dagda. It went straight to voice mail so I left a brief message asking him to call me as soon as he could, then hung up. "I'll tell Amy. At least she'll have the comfort of knowing that her mistake led to discovering a murderer. How long ago did it happen, did they tell you?"

Yes, about thirteen years, so maybe there are others still out there. Owen apparently was keeping a lot of secrets that Vera never knew about.

I thanked her and asked her to bring me any more information if it should come up. As I headed back into the kitchen, Rowan was back to stirring a pot of something on the stove, while Granny sliced a black root that had crimson flesh inside. Amy had dried her eyes and was eating a sandwich.

"I have some news that—" My phone rang and I picked up. It was Dagda.

"Is the antidote ready?" he blurted out. "We've got the town barricaded. Unfortunately, it's going to be difficult to keep people fenced in for too long."

"No, Granny and Rowan are working on it. But I have news for you. Vera isn't Owen's first victim."

That got everybody's attention. Rowan, Granny, and Amy were staring at me.

"What are you talking about?" He sounded so tired that I dreaded adding to his stress, but he had to know.

"Owen's stashed the bodies of two teenagers he raped and murdered out in his garden. Vera met their ghosts after she died." I ticked off the highlights and then promised I'd text him all the pertinent information.

"Oh, good gods. All right. Just tell them to get a move on with the juice, would you?"

I glanced over at Granny. "How long till it's done?"

"About an hour. People will only need a teaspoonful."

"They have to drink it? No shots?" I asked.

"No shots and yes, they need to drink it. Like cough medicine." Granny wrinkled her nose. "Now let me get on with this. Rowan and I need to focus on the energy and make sure it doesn't get off track. Take Amy in the other room, would you?"

I led Amy into the living room, feeling fretful. There was so much to be done but I didn't seem needed for much at this point. I couldn't help Granny and Rowan without messing up the antidote. Owen was already in custody. Colton and I had already caught the hellhound and sent it packing.

"Are you all right?" Amy asked.

I shrugged. "I don't know, to be honest. I'm just…a little adrift, like you are. Different reasons, same basic feeling."

"You could tell me what's going on. It might make you feel better and it would allow me to feel like I'm giving back. I want to feel useful," she said, a pleading tone in her voice. "I'm so sorry I was so rude when I first arrived."

"That's all right." I sighed. "My problem is that I'm used to being active, and I'm not adjusting well to being put on the backburner. I'm used to being the one saving the day. I'm afraid that my patience and my ego aren't holding up very well. It will get better, but right now, I'm just...lost. Like you." I paused as Granny poked her head out of the kitchen.

"We need you, Marquette," was all she said.

I motioned to Amy. "I'll be back." I headed into the kitchen, where Rowan was eyeing me carefully. "What's up?"

"The Aseer told us about your power with the web," Rowan said. "We need your expertise."

"How? What can I do? Is the potion ready?"

Rowan gave it one final stir. "Almost, but there's one thing we still need to do, and neither Granny nor I have the proficiency you do. We need to connect Amy's energy to the energy in the potion. That's the only way that it will fully complete the antidote. Otherwise, it may take care of some of the milder cases, but it won't cure the people who are more seriously affected. The potion has to be linked to the spell caster. Normally, we would have asked Amy to make this potion, which would take care of that, but there's no way we can chance a mistake. We had to make it."

"The Aseer said that you would be able to do this." Granny leaned against the counter.

"Of course I'll help, but I'm not sure exactly how to go about it." I glanced at my phone. "Maybe I should call the Aseer?"

"She said that you had everything necessary to do the job and that you would know how to hook together the energies on the web."

"Let me think for a moment." I sat down and closed my eyes. As I sought for an answer, the memory of being out on the web flashed through my head again, all the strands shimmering against the backdrop of the universe. I was able to touch them and move them, if necessary.

"Bring me a small container of the potion, if you would.

I'll need to touch the outside so don't make it metal if it's still hot."

Granny dished out three ladles of the potion into a plastic container and brought it over, setting it on the table in front of me. I cupped my hands around it. The plastic was warm, but not unbearably so. I closed my eyes, trying to remember how to jump out on the web. And then, before I knew what was happening, I was standing on a long silver thread of my web. I had the container of potion with me, and as I looked at the bowl, I could see thin silver threads leading to both Rowan and Granny.

So *that's* how it worked. Objects were bound to the web as well as people, connected to those people who made them or used them.

I began to search around, looking for Amy's web. I had the feeling I'd recognize it when I saw it, because every single web was a little bit different in resonance. Every web had different colorations to it. My own was tinged with orange and blue. Granny's was a full-blossomed green—as green as the spring leaves on the trees. Rowan's was fiery, with wisps of smoke rising off of the threads.

Forming a picture of Amy in my mind, I willed myself to find her web. I wasn't sure if I was doing it right but I found myself speeding through space, still holding the container.

I landed on another outer thread of my web, where I saw that it connected to another web. As I stared at the place where the threads bonded, I sensed energy off of the web and immediately knew who it belonged to.

The magic was strong that it almost blinded my senses. But it was chaotic, swirling like a vortex. The threads of this web were silver and black, with hints of blue and purple spun into them. And there was sorrow surrounding it, oozing off every thread.

Amy's web. There was so much power and untapped potential that it almost frightened me—she could become a fearsome ally, or enemy.

I looked at the container in my hands, then leaned down. Cautiously taking hold of one of the threads from Amy's web, I gently disconnected it from mine and touched it to the side of the potion container.

"Take hold of this," I whispered.

As I watched, the end of the thread began to bind itself to the potion container.

So that was how it was done. I imagined it would be more difficult if Amy was unwilling to help, but she was more than willing and her threads responded to my command.

I opened my eyes. "I know how to do this."

Taking a deep breath, I stood and walked over to the massive pot that was on the stove. It was easily as big as three regular stock pots. If it only took a few drops for each person, this would be more than enough for the town. "Bring me a stool, please. And a pair of oven mitts. Ask Amy to come into the kitchen."

Rowan brought me the stool while Granny grabbed a couple of oven mitts and handed them to me. She then escorted Amy over to the table and they both sat.

I slid on the mitts, then glanced over at Rowan.

"Would you mind casting a circle? I think it would be strongest if you did so. I want to do this safely in Circle, with all the elements in attendance."

Rowan turned to Granny. "Do you have a knife I could borrow? It needs to be clean and sharp."

"I can get my athame," Granny offered, but Rowan shook her head.

"It would be best if I use a blade that hasn't been bound to someone else. In a pinch, a butcher knife will work. Just as long as it's pointed at the tip."

Granny found her a long knife that was wicked sharp. She

always kept her knives sharp, and told me that the worst thing a chef could do was let their blades grow dull. "It's the best way to get a nasty cut when you're cooking," she had said.

She handed the knife to Rowan, handle first.

Rowan took a few steps away so she wouldn't clip us with it, then held the blade directly out in front of her. She began to turn in a circle and I could feel the energy pouring out of the blade into the air to spread through the house. Rowan was a powerhouse herself, I thought.

I cast this circle once around,
bound by the young Lord and the Maid,
May the energy be strong and sound,
etched into being by this blade.
I cast the circle once again,
bound by the God and Goddess strong
May the energy dance and spin,
May the circle hold ever long.
I cast the circle yet once more,
bound by the Crone and the Sage
May the energy rise and soar
May the magic never fade.

As she finished casting the circle, a hush descended throughout the kitchen. I could feel every tingle of magic that was racing through the room. I took a deep breath and let it out slowly, feeling my muscles unwind. There was something about the energy of magic that relaxed me while heightening my awareness.

Granny took over from there. "Watchtowers of the Earth, I call you. Surround this circle with a ring of rock and stone and bone and crystal. Bring your strength to bear and hold witness to our rites." As she turned, the energy of the earth rose around us to stand as protector.

"Watchtowers of the Air, I call you. Surround this circle with the strength of your winds, your gales blowing away the old and bringing space for the new. Bring your keen insight, and ability to clear away illusion, and hold witness to our rites." A breeze sprang up through the kitchen, sweeping around us, lifting away the gloom and shadows.

"Watchtowers of the Flames, I call you. Surround this circle with the strength of your heat and warmth, burning away infirmity and bringing vigor and strength. Bring with you your powers to heal and hold witness to our rites." Once again, a ripple surrounded the kitchen, only this time it was of warmth—the soothing warmth of gentle sunlight, or of a hearth fire crackling on a cold evening.

"Watchtowers of the Water, I call you. Surround this circle with your crashing ocean waves, washing away anger and misdirection. Bring with you your powers of understanding, and hold witness to our rites." As Granny finished, the cool scent of rain lingered in the air and peace descended around us.

It was my turn to act. I turned back to the pot on the stove, gingerly testing out the oven mitts against the sides. The burner had been off for a while but the pot was still hot, and the mitts protected my hands to where I could clasp hold of the sides without burning myself.

I close my eyes once again, and—surrounded by the protection of the circle and the elements—I lowered myself into a deep trance. As the energy spiraled, I followed it into the potion. I could sense the resonance of each individual herb and root that had gone into the potion, as well as the crystals and stones that had lent their energy to the plants. I could sense Rowan's energy attached to it, and Granny's, and I leaned forward so that my face hovered over the pot.

"Take me out on the web," I whispered.

Within seconds, I went spiraling out of my body to land in the center of my web.

This time I was on the astral for real. As far as the eye could see the universe was filled with webs, one touching the next, everything interconnected by those silver strands.

The energy of the potion was now attached to me as well as to Rowan and Granny. I willed myself to the edges of Amy's web, now that I knew where to look.

As I traveled, I passed web after web, wondering who they belonged to. I was tempted to stop and look in on some of them, especially the ones that flared brighter than others. Some were so brilliant they almost blinded me and I knew they must be powerful witches. Others were faint, fading quickly—the webs of those who were dying. It was hard to ignore them, hard to not try to offer them strength, but that wasn't my place.

I looked around at the hundreds of webs surrounding me. And beyond stretched the rest of the universe, filled with shining threads from top to bottom. If I went out far enough I could find other creatures from other planets, but as much as that fascinated me, right now it was all about Amy and the potion and thinking about the people she had infected.

I kept Amy in the forefront of my thoughts and before long I was standing on the edge of her web. Only this time, she was in the middle of it. I approached her, and her eyes widened.

"What are you doing out here?"

"I need to attach the potion to your energy, so that it can't misfire. Will you help me?"

She nodded, but at that moment, she began to sway dangerously. The scene shifted and she was standing at the top of a massively tall tree, a fir that buckled and waved in the wind. She was clinging for dear life to the top branch, trying not to fall.

I knew it was a metaphor for her emotional state right now, but I needed her to be strong and focused. "You need to come down from there. You have to make the decision to climb down."

"I want to, but I'm afraid," she called down to me.

"You have to be the one to climb down. It has to be your choice."

Slowly, she slid one foot down to the next branch as she hugged the tree. Once again I encouraged her to continue and she struggled, slip sliding to the next branch. She was clearly terrified, but if I could keep her engaged long enough, I could have her down without incident.

Finally, she was a mere twenty feet above me, but the branches ended there. She would have to jump or use the trunk like a fire pole. Either way, her landing was bound to be difficult.

"Just one more step. I know it's scary, but you aren't going to hurt yourself. Your body is safe at home in my kitchen, so take a deep breath and jump. I'll be here and I'll keep you from falling out of your web." I wasn't exactly sure how I was going to manage the promise, but I knew in my heart that I could do it.

Amy resisted, crying and shaking, but I persevered.

"I promise that you won't get hurt. We need you, Amy. I can't come up to get you. You have to do this on your own. Remember, you wanted to help? This is how you can do it."

Her sobs subsiding, Amy crouched, staring at the ground below. "Will I fall through the strands?"

I shook my head. "No more than a spider falls out of their own web. Jump toward me and I'll catch you."

And then, Amy took a deep breath and leapt out at the tree, falling directly toward me. I stepped back but kept my arms out and, as she landed, I grabbed hold of her and held tight. She shifted, steadying her balance.

"All right, I want you to put your hands on the side of this pot with me. It won't hurt you because you are doing it out of body. I'm wearing oven mitts because I actually *do* have my hands on the pot. I want you to infuse as much of your energy into this potion as possible."

Amy closed her eyes, and I felt her power pulsate as she poured it into the stockpot. The potion began to bubble and glisten, and I could tell that it was sucking up her offering, infusing its magic with hers. A few moments later, and every drop that was within the pot sang with her energy, promising renewal and an end to the virus.

I let out a deep breath. "I think you've done it. I think it's ready. You can go back to your body now." I gave her a little push and she vanished. While she was still connected to her web, she was no longer with me on the astral. I took another long look at the potion and—sensing it was complete—I, too, jumped off of the web and landed hard back into my body.

CHAPTER EIGHTEEN

*W*e quickly bottled up the potion in plastic jugs so that they wouldn't break. I call Dagda and he sent some men over to pick it up. He tagged along, and while his men were loading the jugs of potion into their squad cars in coolers to prevent them from spilling, we explained to him how to administer it. We already had taken our doses.

"Each person gets one teaspoon. Not tablespoon, but *teaspoon*. Rowan is going to talk to the Department of Health officials, and explain to them what needs to be done. You're going with them," Granny said, turning to me.

"Me?"

"Yes, and I'll tell you why. What we didn't tell you was that, while you were down at Dagda's office, Rowan contacted the Court Magika."

"Oh?" I asked.

"Yes, and because you worked for the Crown Magika, they've given you a special license so that you have the authority to make the rules regarding this situation. The Department of Health for Terameth Lake will *have* to follow your orders."

"I suggest you get dressed in whatever looks like the most official witch gear you own. Do you have a formal ritual dress?" Rowan held up the badge, which she had printed out at the behest of the Court Magika.

I definitely hadn't foreseen this. "I do have a ritual dress, but you'll have to get it." I told Granny where it was and she headed upstairs. While she was gone, I turned to Rowan. "You really *can* pull strings, can't you?"

"It wasn't that difficult, given your reputation. I talked to your former boss—Royal Jackson—and he had nothing but good things to say about you. When I explained what was going on, he made a suggestion that I think you might want to consider."

There was something afoot. I could see it in her eyes. "What kind of a suggestion?"

"He suggested that you become an official envoy for the Crown Magika, based here in Terameth Lake. Given that we know there are still members of the Covenant of Chaos around, and that there are most likely rogue vampires hiding out, along with the fact that Terameth Lake is sitting directly on Hell's Thicket, which seems to house a portal to dangerous places... Well, it might be a good idea to have someone capable of sending in regular reports on the situation. Royal wants to talk to you about salary and compensation on Monday. I wrote down his contact information in case you don't have it anymore."

Stunned, I sat there speechless. I had no clue what to say, but my thoughts were interrupted when Granny returned with my dress. I limped into her room and changed clothes, forgoing the witchy ankle boots for a pair of sturdy snow boots. Granny joined me, as well as Dominique.

"What do you think about all of this?" I asked. "So much has happened in the past couple days. I feel like I stepped into a crossroads."

"That's because you have," Granny said. "I think you should seriously consider their offer. You'd still be here, with me, but you'd be working at a job that you loved again. I know it wouldn't be the same, you wouldn't be out chasing down vampires, but you'd be keeping track of things and you'd be the one in charge of a division."

I turned to her. "What do you mean, a division? Rowan didn't say anything about that."

"I have a touch of prognostication myself, and I can tell you right now you will be running an office. Not a secretary, but *in charge* of an office. Hell, you could probably hire Colton. He'd make a good agent, don't you think? Though he might want to keep writing. I don't know."

My thoughts were in a whirl as Granny braided my hair into a fancy hairstyle. I wasn't sure how I felt about going back to the Crown Magika, although Granny was right. I wouldn't be a secretary, and *I'd* be the one in charge. Given the fact that my disability was permanent, and I couldn't run around town much, it made sense. And if I was honest with myself, I missed the prestige that came from working for the Crown Magika.

"I'll think about it," I said. "I mean it."

I think you should do it, Dominique said. *This is right up your alley.*

I told Granny what Dominique had said.

She nodded. "My nanny was always a wise woman, even though I didn't want to admit it when I was younger. All right, you look fit to take on the Department of Health." She pinned my badge to my dress. "Remember, attitude is everything."

Nodding, I made my way out to the living room. Dagda held out his arm and escorted me to the police cruiser. He would drive me down and back. As we sat in the car, he shook his head and laughed.

"I heard what they said. Take the job. We can use someone who has your knowledge and who can pull some strings. *I* could use your help. Our fates seem destined to intertwine."

"I guess they do," I said. I flashed him a warm smile, glancing down at the badge. "I suppose this will force people to come get the antidote."

"Not only that, but with your authority, we can institute a door-to-door campaign. And if you do spin it as an antidote, I'm pretty sure we won't encounter too many holdouts. So," he added, "what do we do about Amy?"

"The Aseer wants to work with her on her powers. And if I had the authority of the Crown Magika, I could spin a story that doesn't put her in the wrong. I think I wouldn't mind training her to be an agent. I could use someone with her powers if I'm going to take this job."

"Oh, you're going to take the job, all right. I may not be a fortuneteller, but I'm observant. I have to be because I'm a cop. And I know you want to. Don't let your ego throw this away, Marquette. Don't let your resentment or anger stop you from making a choice that you'll probably end up loving."

All the way down to the station I thought about what he said. Dagda and I had come to a mutual respect, even though I didn't agree with him on much. But he was right.

I wanted something to do, I wanted a focus that could hold me in its grasp, that I could sink my teeth into. Granny's store was wonderful, and I'd always help her out with it. But this would give me what I needed to round out my life. This would give me purpose again.

I also realized that I was grateful that I wouldn't have to leave Terameth Lake. I had resisted leaving the agency, and I had fought and screamed every step of the way, but for the first time in my life, I had a home base. I was making friends here—friends who wouldn't desert me. And I was grateful to be in touch with Granny again.

This way, I could have the best of both worlds.

"I promise I won't let my past interfere with my present. But for now we have a community of people to vaccinate. Or, rather, detoxify. I suppose I better think of the way I'm going to phrase it to the DOH when we get there."

Dagda laughed again and it felt good to hear him pulling out of the funk he'd been in. "While you're thinking, let's pull through an espresso stand and grab us a couple of lattes and doughnuts. What do you say to that?"

"I say, that sounds like the perfect idea." And I meant every word of it.

COMING SOON:

Moonshadow Bay Series: January Jaxson returns to the quirky town of Moonshadow Bay after her husband dumps her and steals their business, and within days she's working for Conjure Ink, a paranormal investigations agency, and exploring the potential of her hot new neighbor. Book eight, **Witch's Web**, is available now, and book nine, **Cursed Web** is available for preorder! Begin with **Starlight Web**.

Night Queen Series: Meet Lyrical, one of the Leannan Sidhe. A displaced princess, Lyrical is working for the newly revamped Wild Hunt Agency in **Tattered Thorns**. Book two and three are available for preorder: **Shattered Spells** and **Fractured Flowers** are available for preorder.

You can find out about the progress of all my series on my **State of the Series page**.

For all of my work, both published and upcoming releases, see the Bibliography at the end of this book, or check out my website at **Galenorn.com** and be sure and sign up for my

newsletter to receive news about all my new releases. Also, you're welcome to join my **YouTube Channel** community.

QUALITY CONTROL: This work has been professionally edited and proofread. If you encounter any typos or formatting issues ONLY, please contact me through my **website** so they may be corrected. Otherwise, know that this book is in my style and voice and editorial suggestions will not be entertained. Thank you.

PLAYLIST

I often listen to music when I write, and CHARMED TO DEATH is no exception. Here's the playlist for the book:

- **A.J. Roach:** Devil May Dance
- **AC/DC:** Back in Black; Dirty Deeds Done Dirt Cheap; Hells Bells
- **Adele:** Rumour Has It
- **Air:** Moon Fever; Surfing on a Rocket
- **Airstream:** Electra
- **Alanis Morissette:** You Oughta Know; Hand in My Pocket; Uninvited; All I Really Want; Eight Easy Steps
- **Alice Cooper:** I'm the Coolest; Didn't We Meet; Welcome to My Nightmare; Some Folks
- **Android Lust:** Here & Now; Saint Over
- **Animotion:** Obsession
- **Arch Leaves:** Nowhere to Go
- **Asteroid Galaxy Tour:** The Sun Ain't Shining No More; The Golden Age; Around the Bend;

Sunshine Coolin'; Bad Fever; Major; Heart Attack; Out of Frequency; Hurricane
- **Band of Skulls:** I Know What I Am
- **Billy Idol:** White Wedding
- **Blondie:** Fade Away and Radiate; Heart of Glass; I Know But I Don't Know; One Way or Another; Call Me; Rapture; Little Caesar
- **Bob Seger & the Silver Bullet Band:** Old Time Rock & Roll; Turn the Page
- **Bobbie Gentry:** Ode to Billie Joe
- **Broken Bells:** The Ghost Inside
- **Camouflage Nights:** (It Could Be) Love
- **Crazy Town:** Butterfly
- **David Bowie:** Golden Years; Fame; Jean Jeanie
- **Devon Cole:** W.I.T.C.H.
- **Dizzi:** Dizzi Jig; Dance of the Unicorns; Galloping Horse
- **DJ Shah:** Mellomaniac
- **Eastern Sun:** Beautiful Being
- **Eels:** Souljacker Part 1
- **Elton John:** Honky Cat; Goodbye Yellow Brick Road; Saturday Night's Alright for Fighting; Rocket Man; Bennie and the Jets; Crocodile Rock
- **Eurythmics:** Sweet Dreams
- **Fats Domino:** I Want to Walk You Home
- **FC Kahuna:** Hayling
- **Fleetwood Mac:** The Chain; Gold Dust Woman
- **Godsmack:** Voodoo
- **Gordon Lightfoot:** Sundown
- **Gorillaz:** Demon Days; Hongkongaton
- **The Guess Who:** American Woman; No Sugar Tonight/New Mother Nature
- **Halsey:** Castle; Haunting

- **Heart:** Magic Man; White Lightning & Wine; Crazy on You; Dreamboat Annie
- **Imagine Dragons:** Natural
- **Jay Price:** The Devil's Bride; Dark-Hearted Man; Coming for You Baby
- **Jeannie C. Riley:** Harper Valley PTA
- **Jefferson Airplane:** She Has Funny Cars; Somebody to Love; 3/5 of a Mile in 10 Seconds; White Rabbit; Plastic Fantastic Lover
- **John Fogerty:** The Old Man Down the Road
- **Johnny Otis:** Willy & The Hand Jive
- **Kirsty MacColl:** In These Shoes?
- **Led Zeppelin:** When the Levee Breaks; Kashmir; Ramble On; The Battle of Evermore; Immigrant Song
- **Loreena McKennitt:** The Mummers Dance; Marco Polo; All Souls Night; The Lady of Shalott
- **Low:** Witches; Plastic Cup; Half-Light
- **Marconi Union:** First Light; Alone Together; Flying; Always Numb; On Reflection; Broken Colours; We Travel; Weightless
- **Mark Lanegan:** The Gravedigger's Song; Riot in My House; Phantasmagoria Blues; Wedding Dress; Methamphetamine Blues
- **Mark Lanegan/Duke Garwood:** Pentacostal; War Memorial; Mescalito; Death Rides a White Horse
- **Matt Corby:** Breathe
- **Nancy Sinatra:** These Boots Are Made for Walking
- **Nick Cave & The Bad Seeds:** Do You Love Me; Red Right Hand
- **Nik Ammar & Marla Altschuler:** Hollywood

- **Nirvana:** Lithium; Heart Shaped Box; Come As You Are; Lake of Fire; All Apologies; On a Plain; Plateau; You Know You're Right
- **Oingo Boingo:** Dead Man's Party; Elevator Man; Return of the Dead Man
- **Orgy:** Social Enemies; Blue Monday
- **PJ Harvey:** The Words That Maketh Murder; In the Dark Places; C'mon Billy; Down by the Water
- **Red Venom:** Let's Get It On
- **Robert Palmer:** Addicted to Love; Simply Irresistible
- **Robin Schulz:** Sugar
- **The Rolling Stones:** Gimme Shelter; 19th Nervous Breakdown; Mother's Little Helper; Jumpin' Jack Flash; Sympathy for the Devil; What a Shame; The Spider and the Fly
- **Rue du Soleil:** We Can Fly; Le Française; Wake Up Brother; Blues Du Soleil
- **Sarah McLachlan:** Possession
- **Screaming Trees:** All I Know; Dime Western
- **Shriekback:** Underwater Boys; And the Rain; The King in the Tree; The Shining Path; Intoxication; Over the Wire; New Man; Go Bang; Big Fun; Dust and a Shadow; Agony Box; Now These Days Are Gone
- **St. Vincent:** Pay Your Way in Pain; Down and Out Downtown; Los Ageless
- **Steppenwolf:** Born to Be Wild; Magic Carpet Ride
- **Talking Heads:** Life During Wartime; Take Me to the River; Burning Down the House; Swamp; Psycho Killer; I Zimbra; Moon Rocks
- **Tamaryn:** While You're Sleeping, I'm Dreaming; Violet's in a Pool

- **The Temptations:** Papa Was a Rolling Stone
- **Tom Petty:** Mary Jane's Last Dance
- **Trills:** Speak Loud
- **The Verve:** Bitter Sweet Symphony
- **Zero 7:** In the Waiting Line

BIOGRAPHY

New York Times, *Publishers Weekly*, and *USA Today* bestselling author Yasmine Galenorn writes urban fantasy and paranormal romance, and is the author of over eighty books, including the Wild Hunt Series, the Fury Unbound Series, the Bewitching Bedlam Series, the Indigo Court Series, and the Otherworld Series, among others. She's also written nonfiction metaphysical books. She is the 2011 Career Achievement Award Winner in Urban Fantasy, given by RT Magazine. Yasmine has been in the Craft since 1980, is a shamanic witch and High Priestess. She describes her life as a blend of teacups and tattoos. She lives in Kirkland, WA, with her husband Samwise and their cats. Yasmine can be reached via her website at **Galenorn.com**. You can find all her links at her **LinkTree**.

Indie Releases Currently Available:

Moonshadow Bay Series:
    Starlight Web
    Midnight Web

Conjure Web
Harvest Web
Shadow Web
Weaver's Web
Crystal Web
Witch's Web
Cursed Web

Magic Happens Series:
Shadow Magic
Charmed to Death

Night Queen Series:
Tattered Thorns
Shattered Spells
Fractured Flowers

Hedge Dragon Series:
The Poisoned Forest
The Tangled Sky

The Wild Hunt Series:
The Silver Stag
Oak & Thorns
Iron Bones
A Shadow of Crows
The Hallowed Hunt
The Silver Mist
Witching Hour
Witching Bones
A Sacred Magic
The Eternal Return
Sun Broken
Witching Moon

Autumn's Bane
Witching Time
Hunter's Moon
Witching Fire
Veil of Stars
Antlered Crown

Lily Bound Series
Soul Jacker

Chintz 'n China Series:
Ghost of a Chance
Legend of the Jade Dragon
Murder Under a Mystic Moon
A Harvest of Bones
One Hex of a Wedding
Holiday Spirits
Well of Secrets
Chintz 'n China Books, 1 – 3: Ghost of a Chance,
Legend of the Jade Dragon, Murder Under A
Mystic Moon
Chintz 'n China Books, 4-6: A Harvest of Bones,
One Hex of a Wedding, Holiday Spirits

Whisper Hollow Series:
Autumn Thorns
Shadow Silence
The Phantom Queen

Bewitching Bedlam Series:
Bewitching Bedlam
Maudlin's Mayhem
Siren's Song
Witches Wild

Casting Curses
Demon's Delight
Bedlam Calling: A Bewitching Bedlam Anthology
The Wish Factor (a prequel short story)
Blood Music (a prequel novella)
Blood Vengeance (a Bewitching Bedlam novella)
Tiger Tails (a Bewitching Bedlam novella)

Fury Unbound Series:
Fury Rising
Fury's Magic
Fury Awakened
Fury Calling
Fury's Mantle

Indigo Court Series:
Night Myst
Night Veil
Night Seeker
Night Vision
Night's End
Night Shivers
Indigo Court Books, 1-3: Night Myst, Night Veil, Night Seeker (Boxed Set)
Indigo Court Books, 4-6: Night Vision, Night's End, Night Shivers (Boxed Set)

Otherworld Series:
Moon Shimmers
Harvest Song
Blood Bonds
Otherworld Tales: Volume 1
Otherworld Tales: Volume 2

For the rest of the Otherworld Series, see website at **Galenorn.com.**

Bath and Body Series (originally under the name India Ink):
  Scent to Her Grave
  A Blush With Death
  Glossed and Found

Misc. Short Stories/Anthologies:
  Once Upon a Kiss (short story: Princess Charming)
  Once Upon a Curse (short story: Bones)
  Once Upon a Ghost (short story: Rapunzel Dreaming)
  The Longest Night (A Pagan Romance Novella)

Magickal Nonfiction: A Witch's Guide Series.
  Embracing the Moon
  Tarot Journeys
  Totem Magick

Printed in Great Britain
by Amazon

23058543R00119